ROGUE FAE

Shadow Fae—Book Seven

C.N. CRAWFORD

Corey Press

For my little boy Ronan, who is beginning to learn the magic of how hands work.

If man were a beast or an angel, he would not be able to be in dread, and the greater the dread the greater the man.

— SØREN KIERKEGAARD

A donis handed me a canteen of water. Sunlight filtered through the laurel leaves, sparking in his pale eyes. Above us, Drakon—his dragonile—swooped between the tree branches.

"See?" Adonis said. "I remember things about you. You need to drink water to stay alive. I may have even packed you and Hazel sandwiches."

I took the canteen gratefully from him. "Your understanding of biology astounds me." I cocked my head. "What did you put in the sandwiches?"

"Bread with strawberries and butter. And a little pepper."

I quirked a smile. Adonis had no idea how food worked. "That is weird as hell, but it sounds strangely delicious." Much like him, in fact.

It was sweet of him, anyway. Unfortunately, we weren't alone, or I might have kissed him right then.

Muriel, an angel friend of his we'd just met this morning, was staring right at us. "I'm just concerned that Ruby and Hazel are slowing us down." She delivered this declaration to my sister and me in a sickly sweet tone, batting her eyelids.

Adonis shot her a sharp look. "Don't be ridiculous, Muriel. We're making good time."

I glared at her. Ostentatious diamonds glittered from her wrists and from her blond curls. They were probably real, but her smile was fake as dollar-store rhinestones. Everything about her annoyed me, to the point where I nearly forgot about the fact that we were probably on our way to be slaughtered.

Adonis had arranged to meet the Horseman of Conquest to discuss an alliance. Kratos had chosen the location. Did I trust him? Hell no, I didn't trust him. Hence, I'd brought my bow and arrows with me.

I had a strong feeling Kratos had set a trap for us. And yet, Adonis seemed to think this meeting was our only chance to win in a war against the two evil horsemen. The ones who were just about ready to cleanse the rest of the earth of every human, fae, and demon.

I screwed the top back on the canteen. "Let's just keep going, shall we?"

Muriel cast an irritated glance over her shoulder. "No offense, but I don't think we need the fae. Sometimes powerful forces take on dead weight, and that's bad for everyone. We all know animals get overtired easily."

Adonis halted his march over the forest floor, and I nearly ran into his back. At the look he was giving Muriel, a chill rippled over my skin. Even *he* was about to lose it with his old friend.

"Sorry." She blew me a kiss. "I forgot the fae can be sensitive about being called animals. But people should just accept what they are, right? Just like I've accepted that I'm divine. Right, my darlings?"

Muriel had a way of unleashing the most brutal commentary with kisses and terms of endearment that made my skin crawl.

Hazel seemed amazingly unperturbed by Muriel's attitude. She ignored the insults, lazily threading a string of leaves together as she walked.

Clenching my jaw, I started marching again, and the others moved along with me. Even though I was trying to keep my cool, the gemstones in my forehead were heating up, ready to claim some angel life.

"Just so we're clear," I snarled. "I've infiltrated the fortresses of two horsemen. I stole the gemstones from Aereus *and* the Old Gods, blocked the Heavenly Host from the earth with a magic blue shield, and I rescued Adonis from the underworld. And I'm the Bringer of Light."

"I don't even know what that is." She wrinkled her nose. "And the Heavenly Host broke through that crappy shield you made, then disappeared somewhere on earth, so, I'm not super impressed with your powers." She sighed, flicking her eyes to the heavens like a martyr. "Look, there's no reason to get upset with me, sweetie. I dedicate my life to helping people. I ask for nothing in return."

Annoying as she was, she had a point about the Heavenly Host. The shield I'd created to block the angels from the earth had only been temporary. Now, we were on borrowed time before the angels destroyed the rest of the earth, and all of my attempts to create new shields had failed miserably.

Ever since I'd stolen the gemstones, I'd had the feeling that the Old Gods didn't really want me using their powers. Believe me, I'd been trying to master my new skills over the past few days. My life—maybe everyone's life—depended on it. But each time I tried to summon the magic of the Old Gods, it seemed like the magic would kill me. I'd actually spent an entire week in an empty field outside Adonis's castle trying to conjure a new shield, and each time my magic intensified, it had felt as if my body was about to blow apart with the force of their rage, and I could no longer focus. Since I'd stolen the gemstones, I'd completely lost control of the magic.

If I had to guess, the Old Gods didn't take too kindly to thievery. And worse, I thought they might want me dead now, but I kept that last part to myself. I was supposed to be the earth's only hope. It wouldn't do any good to extinguish hope, right? I'd just have to work at my powers, until they didn't kill me.

"Let's just keep going, shall we?" I snapped. "We don't want to be late for Kratos's slaughter party." I'd only known Muriel for a few hours, but already I wanted to fling her into the gorge.

Still, as much as I'd like to see her perfect body tumble down the rugged slope—slamming against every jagged rock on the way—she had a purpose here. Muriel was a bridge between Kratos and Adonis. In fact, she'd known them both for a thousand years or so. She was supposed to function as some sort of mediator in our negotiations. If either Kratos or Adonis tried to pull any shit, Muriel would use her angel powers to keep them in line.

Apparently, they both trusted her, even though she was clearly an asshole.

"How long have you two known each other, anyway?" My voice sounded a little too sharp as I glared at her.

"For centuries, sweetie. Adonis was there to help me when I nearly fell from grace."

"Oh?" At last, Muriel was starting to seem interesting.

"Centuries ago," she said. "In London. A wickedly beautiful incubus seduced me. Only Adonis's magic was able to pull me back from eternal ruination." She shuddered. "I'd started to grow horns. Like a demon. Revolting."

These angels and their abstinence. It really was a sad waste of life.

A languid sigh escaped Muriel. "Such young creatures, these two little fae."

"How old are you, anyway?" asked Hazel.

Muriel stretched her arms over her head. "Older than Adonis. I was there when Eve ate the fruit in the Garden of Eden."

Hazel scrunched her nose. "Wait—the Garden of Eden is real? I thought that was just a myth, like alligators who live in sewers and plants that give you rashes."

"Plants can give you rashes." I scowled at the leaves in her grip. "Hazel, that's poison ivy."

"Whoops." She dropped them on the ground, wiping her hands on her jeans.

"And the Garden of Eden was real," Adonis added. "Only it wasn't an apple that Eve ate. It was a grape."

Hazel frowned. "Well, grapes don't grow on trees, so there are holes in your story already."

Muriel stared at her nails. "I don't see what was so great about the Garden, anyway. Nature's boring."

Another reason why Muriel was dumb as rocks. Right now, we were walking through a sylvan paradise, and she couldn't even see it. Edible mushrooms grew along the forest floor, and ripe hawthorn berries and rose hips grew from the shrubs around us. Drakon swooped through the cherry trees above us, his teeth stained with the fruit. There was a banquet here for those who knew where to look. Forget Eden. *This* was Paradise—nature was the church of the gods.

My gaze flicked to the left of the path, where chinks of sunlight flecked a simple cottage. It looked like it had just been built since the Great Nightmare began.

Smoke curled from the chimney, rising between the gnarled boughs of an oak. Through the window, I caught a glimpse of a woman stirring something in a pot over a fireplace. Soup, I imagined. When she tucked a strand of her platinum hair behind her ear, I realized her ears were pointed. A fae—just like me. I stared as a fae male came up behind her, planting a kiss on her cheek.

That's what I'm missing. Living out here in nature like the fae were supposed to. A simple life, surrounded by the paradise of nature.

"A little fae cottage," said Muriel. "How quaint. Until they go feral and eat each other."

I blocked her out, already envisioning my life in a cottage like that. I'd hunt deer and drink ice-cold water from a forest stream.... Adonis would wear nothing but a fig leaf. At night, we would sit in front of the fire sipping home brews, eating soup. Then, he'd push me up against an oak tree, grab my thighs, and—

"Ruby," said Hazel. "You're about to walk into a tree."

My eyes snapped open, and I stopped short of a laurel trunk. "I know what I'm doing," I muttered.

"What were you thinking about?" asked Hazel.

I cleared my throat. "Nothing. Just the upcoming meeting with Kratos. I was thinking about our best strategy."

Ugh. Weird that the vision had been so potent. I was beginning to suspect that the stones I'd stolen from the Old Gods might be messing with my head a little. These days, my fantasies—my phantom life—sometimes seemed more vibrant than the real world.

Or—it was possibly the fact that Adonis and I had been separated for a week after I saved him from the underworld, and now I couldn't stop staring at his muscled body. For a full week, he'd been away, trying to make contact with Kratos.

"Are you nervous for this meeting?" asked Hazel. "What if it's an ambush? What if Kratos is just luring us into a trap?"

"I certainly don't trust Kratos. But we have Adonis on our side, and if it comes down to an angel battle, I like his odds."

As I looked at Adonis's perfect body, it occurred to me

that maybe the problem with temptation in the Garden of Eden had nothing to do with Eve. From my perspective, everything was the angels' fault. If I had to guess, Azazeyl—the angel who tempted Eve—was a stone-cold hottie. And when she ate the grapes he offered her, Paradise was lost. Not her fault, even though it did ruin everything for everyone.

Azazeyl cursed humanity with the ability to speak—and with language came neurosis. Adam and Eve were no longer simply cavorting through the plants and screwing up against oak trees. After the fall, they were thinking about things like *What is death, and what happens to your soul when you die? Does Adam always have to chew with his mouth open? Is there more to life than fig leaves and fruit trees? And is Azazeyl ever coming back here or did I weird him out when I tried to compliment his abs?*

If it weren't for the angels, Adam and Eve and the rest of humanity would have happily stayed in their paradise, neurosis-free.

Angels had screwed up everything.

And now, I'd be relying on these same angels to fix the whole apocalypse they started.

Muriel turned to frown at me. "I've always wondered if the fae take baths or if you just lick yourselves clean like dogs?"

I picked up a clump of earth from the ground and hurled it at Muriel, eliciting a shriek when it hit her white gown.

"That's cats, dipshit," I shouted.

Since the world's fate depended on it, it was a good thing I had a natural rapport with these angels.

❧ 2 ❧

The cave's entrance didn't look like much—a four-foot-tall hole that opened from the side of a vine-covered rock. Tree roots grew around it, and Adonis had to crouch to fit through the opening.

Muriel followed right behind him, close enough to be all up in his metaphorical fig leaves.

I crawled on my hands and knees into the cave. After a few feet, the passage opened up enough that I could stand.

Muriel spoke a few words in Angelic, and a glowing orb appeared above her, casting warm light over smooth stone walls.

"What is this place?" asked Hazel.

"Once, these caves were used by the Templars," said Adonis. "They built them as a place to worship the gods in secret. If the Inquisition had found these temples, they would have burned the Templars."

"Like they did in France," added Muriel.

My eyes roamed over the carvings on the walls—the Angelic script and alchemical symbols—stars, kings, two men riding a horse.

As we walked deeper into the caves, the walls became rougher and the pictures more primitive. The carvings changed—no longer words, but now thorny vines and gnarled boughs of trees, the lines increasingly crude and violent. Somehow, it seemed like we were walking back in time.

In these ancient caverns, a shiver rippled over me. Kratos had chosen an isolated place for this meeting point.

"You're sure he doesn't want to trap us here?" I whispered.

"We had to take a risk," said Adonis. "He insisted on meeting on his terms."

"Sure," I said. "That doesn't sound suspicious at all."

"I thought you had goddess powers," said Muriel.

"Yep." *It's just that they'll kill me, so I'm not eager to use them.*

"Anyway," Muriel continued. "If I know anything about Kratos, it's that he's serious about having the horseman curse removed. The man has been desperate to make love to a woman for thousands of years. Only you can make that happen."

"What an honor," I said. "I'm like a cosmic wingman."

At last, the tunnel opened into a large cavern, and my heart sped up at the sight of Kratos. He stood alone, his coppery wings swooping behind him. Always, at the first sight of Kratos, I had the strongest urge to drop to my knees, his power of conquest washing over me. I wanted to lower my eyes, to sink to the ground. Still, I fought the urge, forcing myself to keep his gaze.

The candlelight wavered over his masculine features, his eyes blazing like sunlight.

It took me a moment to realize that someone else had come with him—Elan, the fae servant from his castle. Elan smiled at me, nervously tugging on the hem of his cat sweater. I smiled back at him. With tension thick in the air, it felt good to see a friendly face.

"Kratos," said Adonis. His dark magic whipped around

him with an air of menace. I had to wonder if he did that on purpose, like a cat raising his hackles to seem more threatening. "I received your missive."

"Do you have news about Aereus and Johnny?" asked Kratos.

Adonis shook his head. "Only that they've joined forces at Sadeckrav Castle. Are you committed to joining an alliance with us? As allies, we might be able to combat the other horsemen while Ruby fights the Heavenly Host. As soon as we find them."

Kratos stared at me. "Remove the curse from me, and I'm on your side."

I tried not to think about the fact that if I pulled his curse off him, the first thing he'd be doing was trying to get laid. That was his own business.

I took a step closer to him, letting my gaze become unfocused until I could see the dark magic of the curse writhing around his neck. "Are you ready for this?"

"I'm stiff with anticipation."

I narrowed my eyes. Was it just me, or was that a double entendre?

"I'm ready to thrust myself deeply into my new life," he continued. "Until I reach the fulfillment I've always been seeking."

He *had* to be doing this on purpose. He looked dead serious, though.

I pushed those thoughts out of my mind and stared at the magic swirling around his neck. With the curse removed, Kratos would no longer have to follow the demands of the Heavenly Host—to hunt humans, to force them into submission. He'd no longer have to worry about falling from grace if he indulged in pleasure.

In short, I had the power to free him completely.

The stones in my forehead began to warm, and the

ancient power of the Old Gods began to thrum over my body as I prepared to pull the curse off him.

Except—another, otherworldly power was mingling with my own. A deep, uncontrolled rage built in my chest, making it hard for me to focus. My stomach growled as hunger joined in with fury, starvation and wrath mingling together into primal hangriness.

This meant only one thing. Aereus and Johnny—our enemies—were nearby.

I should've known Kratos would betray us.

I whirled around, meeting Adonis's gaze. "They're here. The others."

Already, Adonis was pulling the sword from his scabbard, the blade glinting in the torchlight. I unslung my bow, nocking an arrow, my grip tense on the bowstring.

Except, as I lifted my bow, my skull filled with a cacophony of voices—angelic voices that echoed inside my mind, confusing my own thoughts. I couldn't remember what I needed to do. The arrow clattered harmlessly on the ground.

From one of the tunnels behind Kratos, angels rushed into the cavern, swords raised. Each of them was chanting in their infernal Angelic language. As they did, rock began to rain from the ceiling. The ground shifted and jerked beneath my feet, and the carvings on the walls seemed to come to life, snapping through the air.

Angelic was the language of creation, and they were using it to mess with us, big time.

Chaos rampaged through my skull until I could no longer hear my own thoughts. Flanking me, Adonis and Kratos were adding their own Angelic chants, bending the universe to their wills. Unfortunately, they were bending my mind with it. Drakon swooped above us, his screeches reverberating in the cavern, adding to the tumult.

For a moment, we were horribly outnumbered. Then, a low growl rumbled across the cavern, and darkness fell. Adonis's dark magic whispered around us, and shadows consumed the cave.

Shouts rang out and light sparked as angels tried to fight the darkness. I dropped to my knees, my hands over my ears, dimly aware of the sounds of clashing swords clanging above the Angelic clatter. Something slithered against my skin, and I opened my eyes to find vines from the walls—come to life and curling around my body like pythons.

The stones in my forehead began to warm up. The magic of the Old Gods simmered in my body, giving me a little strength. I just couldn't let them overwhelm me.... For just a moment, the chaos in my skull went quiet as the light inside me built. *Sweet relief.*

Then, with a burst of strength, I ripped the vines off me. My canines began to lengthen, hands twisting, becoming claws, adrenaline racing through my veins. Feral Ruby was coming out to play, and she was angry as hell.

An angel was upon me, his perfect features twisted in hate, wings spread wide. His sword arced down. I shifted sideways, fast as a snake. I let out a bestial snarl as I pulled my dagger from my belt, thrusting, moving with the blade. It plunged into the angel's belly. His eyes widened in surprise and fear. When I pulled out the dagger, I felt it scrape the angel's ribs. He fell, his wings twisted and broken underneath. He struggled to raise his sword, blood trickling from his lips. I licked my dagger's blade, then kicked him in the face. He gasped, the sword dropping to the ground.

A wild roar escaped my throat, and I snatched his sword from the ground. The next thing I knew, I was carving my blade through the vines that had trapped another fae—an important one. My sister? Instinct compelled me to free her.

The hacked vines dropped from her limbs, and I watched her run away from me.

I tried to think clearly through the haze of my mind, and I whirled to look for my enemy. Wrath consumed me, and I wanted blood. My sword clashed with an angel's, and the music of the Old Gods whispered through my blood, urging me to slaughter the invasive species. *Drive the angels from the earth. Reclaim it for us.*

Somewhere, under the fog of fury, the real Ruby screamed. She wasn't quite in control anymore.

꙰ 3 ꙰

I scanned the cavern. Among the chaos of warring angels, I was looking for my prey—one of the leaders. It took a moment until my gaze landed on the starving one—the one who filled my gut with a gnawing sense of emptiness. The Horseman of Famine.

His eyes widened at the sight of me. Scared. Good. My hunter's instincts roared at the smell of his fear. I needed to cut my way through the other enemies in order to get to him.

I pushed my way through the throng. The angels surrounded me, but they didn't fight well in the cramped space of the cavern. They tried to swing their swords, to spread their wings, impossible moves when bodies are squeezed and mashed together. This was a place to fight dirty. To claw, and bite, and scratch. To fight like a beast. Perfect for me.

I left the sword behind me, carving with the knife. Somewhere along the way, I found a jagged rock, dripping blood. Not mine.

Someone was laughing hysterically. Me, I thought. *The death of angels brings me joy.*

Or was it ... *The Angel of Death brings me joy...?* I wasn't sure which thought made sense.

The Old Gods' light beamed from my ribs, blazing over the cavern. Their magic wanted me to reclaim Paradise. *Kill them all....*

Only problem was, the light magic wanted to drive me from the earth, too. As the magic built inside me, I could feel it tearing cracks in me. It was splintering my ribs, power rising in a wild crescendo. My body was going to explode.

The Horseman of Famine lifted a bow and arrow, but his hands were shaking too much to aim it properly. My magic was affecting him. He shrieked, smoke rising from his starved body. He was trying to save himself, screaming something at me.

Still, I couldn't hear him over the screaming in my own mind. This wasn't right. A creature like me—a beast—was never meant to use divine magic, and it would kill me to use it.

An arrow pierced my flesh, and the sharp stab of pain snapped me out of my haze.

With the agony, the Old Gods' magic began to dim, and I clutched my chest. Even with the pain gripping my body, I was relieved to be free of that powerful force. That shit did *not* feel right.

Johnny loosed another arrow, but I knocked it off its trajectory with a surge of light magic. Instead of hitting me in the heart, it struck me in the shoulder.

I slammed against the rocky earth. Agony rippled down my body. I gritted my teeth, trying to block out the pain. And yet the pain was doing its job, sharpening my mind further as I lay on the ground, clutching my shoulder. I tightened my jaw. Now, the whole situation was crystal clear to me, and it was not ideal.

Johnny was aiming another arrow at me. If it hit my heart,

I'd die. I tried to summon the concentration to unleash another surge of light magic, but the fucker had used iron-tipped arrows, and the metal sapped my powers, poisoning my blood. Our eyes met, and I saw death.

A shriek pierced the air, and Drakon swooped down, knocking Johnny off his perch. I grunted with agony and tore one of the arrows from my body, nearly fainting from the pain. But I couldn't have the iron poisoning my body further. Blood gushed from the open wound. From the ground, I glanced around frantically, looking for my lover.

There!

He was standing up, searching for me. My movements were sluggish, I was dizzy from pain. I couldn't hide, couldn't rush to him. At any second—

Just then, I felt a tingle on the back of my neck. Adonis's dark magic whispered over my skin, soothing the pain. The shadows became thicker around me, giving me cover from the arrows. Shaking, I pushed up onto my hands and knees, sucking in ragged breaths. I crawled away from Johnny.

A burst of light flashed in the cave—one of the angels fighting back against Adonis's shadows. A volley of arrows soared overhead before darkness fell again. Like an animal crawling off to die, I dragged myself into a dark corner of the cave. Pebbles bit into my palms and knees until I leaned against a wall.

Johnny's voice echoed off the cave—Cockney-tinged Angelic spells—and Adonis's dark magic dissipated like smoke.

Raw pain arced through my body once more. I fell back against the wall. Flames rose all around the cave—the angels trying to smoke us out.

In the dancing light of the fire, I could see Adonis locked in a swordfight with Aereus, but I couldn't see my sister through the flames.

"Hazel!" I shouted.

I tried yanking the remaining arrow out of my shoulder, but my hands were shaking too badly. *I can't stand up.*

"Hazel!" I shrieked, panic rising. I couldn't find her.

Flames rose around me, illuminating the cave, and high-pitched screams echoed off the cavern walls. In the smoky haze, I blinked at the sight of an angelic mob pulling Muriel through the dirt—her body beaten, bloodied. A broken bone jutted from her chest, and her head lolled. If she was human, she'd be dead.

I could hear Kratos roaring with fury, glimpsed him briefly slicing his sword through an angel.

Through the chaos of blood and flames, I caught another glimpse of Adonis. His sword clashed with Aereus's. I gasped as I caught sight of Johnny—an arrow trained on Adonis from behind.

"Adonis!" I shouted, trying to move across the cave.

I tried standing, but a stray arrow slammed me in the leg. I screamed, certain my femur was splintering.

When I looked up again, Johnny had already unleashed an arrow, piercing Adonis's heart. Drakon's shrieks were ear-splitting, as if he could feel his master's pain. Horror slammed into me. We were losing.

Get up, Ruby. Godsdamn it, get up.

Pain shot through my body, but I pushed myself up. This wasn't happening. I couldn't let them take Adonis from here. The Devil's Bane on Johnny's arrow had already worked its way into his system, blood staining his clothes, his eyes losing focus.

I shuffled forward, determined to get to him. Aereus—Horseman of War—lifted Adonis from under his shoulders and began dragging Death's body from the cavern. The poison-tipped arrow protruded from Adonis's chest.

I let out a scream of anger and bloodlust, and rushed after

them, but a cluster of angels blocked my way. No, not a cluster. A legion. I would plow through them all. I would.

Someone grabbed my wrist. Snarling, I raised my dagger, about to thrust it into the bastard's neck.

"Ruby!" Kratos roared at me. "We're pulling back!"

"No!"

"Your sister needs you." He waved at her. Hazel was lying on the ground, blinking, confused, blood running from her temple.

Tears of frustration blurred my vision as I hurried to her, helping her stand.

"Through there!" Kratos shouted at me, pointing to a side cavern.

I began to shuffle in the direction of the opening, stumbling, Hazel groaning with pain. A group of angels detached from the host, rushing for us. There were at least a dozen. I was dizzy, weak, desperate.

Kratos raised his sword, his wings spread wide, and lunged at them. The Horseman of Conquest laid waste around him, his sword carving through wings, limbs, and bodies. I turned away, pulling Hazel through the small opening.

And then—darkness.

WHEN I WOKE, AN ANGEL STOOD OVER ME, HIS HEAD haloed by the moon. It took me a moment to realize it was Kratos. Anger slammed into me. The bastard had betrayed us.

Hadn't he?

I pushed myself up onto my elbows, and my chest felt like it was fracturing. It took me a moment to realize the screaming I heard was my own.

Kratos held up a hand. "Easy there. I only took the arrows out a few hours ago."

I clutched my collarbone. Kratos might have pulled the arrows out, but the iron had worked its way into my bloodstream. I felt like I'd been run over by a train. "What's happening, you traitorous fuck?" I gasped. "Where's Hazel?"

"Calm down. She's sleeping." He nodded to his right. "She's fine."

Wincing, I turned my head. She lay in the dirt, curled up by a bonfire. Her chest slowly rose and fell. Elan slept next to her, his gentle snores floating through the air.

"I'm not the enemy," said Kratos.

Maybe. Unlikely.

I'd seen the other angels drag Adonis and Muriel out. What had become of them? A sharp pang of protectiveness welled in my chest. Adonis was the Angel of Death, but I still wanted to keep him safe, and I'd failed. If anyone hurt him, I'd smash their heads into the rocky earth. And right now, Kratos seemed like enemy number one. Probably.

I clenched my jaw. I wasn't exactly in a position to fight right now, but it didn't stop the fury. "You led us into a trap. Johnny and Aereus took Adonis, didn't they?"

His eyes gleamed in the darkness. "I have no idea where they came from. If I'd planned this, do you really think you'd still be here? You were their target. It's why they brought iron. You're the only one who can kill them. The capture of Adonis is just a way to get to you."

None of this made sense. "So how did the other horsemen know about this specific location, then? They knew exactly where we were." As much as I hated Muriel, I didn't think she'd been the leak. I'd seen them drag her battered body out of the place.

"I don't know," said Kratos. "Spies, probably. Watching your movements."

I shook my head. "We took a secure route here. I didn't see any sentinels or cherubs, and believe me, I'm conditioned to notice them."

"I traveled underground, so they wouldn't have seen me."

I glared at him. I was almost certain he'd betrayed us, but I wasn't going to get him to admit it right now. I needed to keep a level head. "Where's Drakon?"

"I have no idea." He didn't really seem to care, either.

Blocking out the sharp pain, I scanned my surroundings. We had camped out in an oak grove. Of the six of us who'd met in the cavern, only four remained. I had a hard time believing either Hazel or Elan had given up our location, which meant Kratos was just playing along with this charade, concealing his real plans.

For now, I'd keep my suspicions to myself. If I was going to uncover the truth, I'd need Kratos to let down his guard.

A wave of dizziness and nausea washed over me, and my head fell back against the earth. The last thing I saw before I lost consciousness again was a faint gleam of moonlight silvering Kratos's unearthly copper wings.

4

I woke in a four-poster bed, moonlight streaming through the windows. I had vague memories of a journey: the scent of cedar wrapped around me, wings rhythmically beating the air as the wind rushed over my body. I'd been flying in Kratos's arms.

Pain still pierced my body. I wanted nothing more than to lie flat on the pillows, minimizing the pain, but I needed to figure out what was going on. When I was a kid, I'd competed in gymnastics tournaments. My dad had been a little intense about it—the only parent screaming on the sidelines. Now, whenever I had to push myself, his voice boomed in my head. *Don't get complacent, Ruby.*

Grimacing, I pushed myself up to look around me. Stone room, tapestries glorifying war, the four-poster bed—I was back in Kratos's castle.

One of the tall, peaked windows was open, and wisteria vines had climbed through it, spreading across the floor like an outstretched hand reaching for me. I lifted my arm, and the vine seemed to strain for me. For the first time, I felt as if

I could *hear* the music of the vines—a faint humming. The sound of the spirit that lived within it.

I strained my eyes in the dim light, examining the rest of the room. Faint, golden light glowed around the doorknob. Angelic magic. If I had to guess, Kratos had locked me in here.

I clutched my chest. This was the first time I'd been here without Adonis, and his absence felt like a hole between my ribs.

Could he still hear my thoughts? I had no idea, and I'd never been able to hear back from him. I breathed deeply, trying to think calmly.

Adonis? I'm going to come for you. Wherever you are.

That was assuming I could get past Kratos and get out of here. What the hell was his plan? Maybe he wanted to take the Bringer of Light out of the equation and join forces with the Heavenly Host. Maybe I was supposed to be his first sexual conquest after I pulled the curse from him.

I had no idea. Whatever the case, I had to get out of here. I might have to kill Kratos, break Hazel free from her imprisonment, and get us the hell out of Hotemet. Find my way to Adonis.

But before I could piece together anything resembling a coherent plan, the doorknob began to turn.

The door creaked open, and my body tensed.

When Hazel's crown of wild black hair poked into the room, I loosed a breath.

"What the hell is going on?" I whispered.

Hazel didn't look particularly concerned about anything. In fact, she was holding a tray of steaming food. My stomach rumbled. Already, my gaze was roaming over the roast chicken and mashed potatoes.

"I'm bringing you dinner," said Hazel. "Thought you'd be hungry."

"Yeah I am, but ... why am I locked in this room? And why don't you seem concerned about it?"

"What do you mean?"

"I can see the magic on the door."

Hazel glanced at the golden light pulsing around the door-knob. "Oh, that? It's not locking you in. It's keeping out anyone but me and him. He doesn't want Johnny coming in to pick your bones out of your body."

I grimaced. "Does everyone know about this bone picking thing?" Despite the topic of conversation, my muscles began to relax. I still didn't trust Kratos, but at least he hadn't trapped me in here against my will. At least, not this time.

I tried to sit up completely, but the ache in my chest had me flat on the pillows again within seconds. "Hazel. This is serious."

"What?"

"I'm gonna need you to feed me that chicken," I said. "And the mashed potatoes, too."

"Ugh, fine."

I heard the sound of a knife scraping against the plate. The next moment, a speared piece of chicken hovered above my mouth. I chewed it thoughtfully, trying to figure out what the hell had happened to us in the Templar cave. A silence fell over the room.

Hazel wouldn't have leaked the info, would she? I mean—she'd said some things about how we were better off being ruled by the horsemen. After her time with the dragons, she'd come back a totally different person than she used to be. Hazel thought that you should always choose the winning side of a war, no matter what the costs. But she wouldn't have turned on her own sister.

Right?

"Are you worried about Adonis?" she asked.

"Yes. I know he won't die. I'm the only one who can kill

him. But I don't want to think about what Aereus the Angel of Torture might be doing with him." In my current state, I wouldn't be able to rescue him, and I didn't want to lose my mind imagining the worst. "I'm going to get him as soon as I can."

"I don't think that will be anytime soon."

Was I the only one who saw the danger we were in? Every day that we let pass was another day the Heavenly Host could come out of hiding and slaughter the rest of the earth's inhabitants. And we didn't even know where to find them. "We don't have much time to fuck around, Hazel. I don't know what the angelic horde is planning, but it's not going to be pretty."

Hazel shoveled a forkful of mashed potatoes into my mouth, and I studied her. Her blasé attitude was a little concerning.

What if Kratos and Hazel were working together? Maybe they were both lying to me, keeping me here until they could take over the world, along with Famine and War.

Ugh. Speaking of losing my mind, I would probably drive myself nuts imagining all the possible scenarios that might destroy the world.

I needed to keep a clear head and speak to Yasmin. It had been far too long since I'd gotten in touch with my handler from the Institute. We could exchange information, and she could help me figure out exactly how to ferret out the leak. Maybe the Institute even had some information I could use.

As soon as I physically could, I'd haul my broken body out of bed and find a way to contact her. I wasn't going to get complacent here in my comfortable bed.

☙❧

Night had fallen in the garden.

A beautiful man approached me—completely naked. His hair hung to his shoulders, and moonlight washed over his perfect body. I recognized him from somewhere—from the statue at Adonis's castle. Azazeyl, the original fallen angel.

He handed me a grape, and I ate it. The sweet, tangy juice burst in my mouth, and as it did, chaos erupted in my mind. My own voice echoed off the inside of my skull—screaming about death, until I no longer knew who I was or what I was doing here. The world collapsed into chaos around me.

My own scream ripped me from my sleep.

I gasped, trying to sit up, but my body still wasn't quite there yet. I'd come a little too close to dying from an iron arrow to the heart, and my mind wasn't letting me forget it. The door slammed open, and I lifted my head just enough to see Kratos rush into the room in a blur of copper.

"What's happening?" he demanded.

To a thousand-year-old horseman of the apocalypse, "I had a bad dream" probably sounded a bit lame. "Just, uh ... just the pain from the arrow wounds. I rolled on my ribs funny."

A brusque nod. "Oh."

I narrowed my eyes at him. The timing of the ambush had been interesting. The other horsemen had busted in right before I could remove his curse—almost as if he was still working with the Heavenly Host, still committed to completing his sacred duty.

"Do you still want your curse removed?" I asked.

He sat at the edge of my bed, his weight compressing the mattress.

"Of course. But we will wait until you've had a chance to heal. The iron still courses through your blood."

How convenient. "Actually, I think I'm on the mend. I want to find Adonis as soon as I can." I could hardly sit up, but these were minor details.

Kratos frowned. "You're in no condition to travel. In any case, Adonis will be fine. The other horsemen can't kill him, and they'll want to use him."

"For what, exactly?"

"To trade for you and Hazel."

My chest tightened. "They want Hazel, too?"

"She's from the same bloodline as you. If you can harness the power of the Old Gods, so can she. But Adonis will be fine. I'm sure they'll torture him within an inch of his life, but—"

"Exactly why we're going after him as soon as we can."

"You can hardly move, Ruby."

Convenient, again. Angels had brought language to the earth. And along with language came the ability to lie.

Blocking out the pain, I forced myself up onto my elbows. "We're running out of time. There's a horde of angels who want to slaughter us and everything else on earth, and you don't seem particularly bothered about it. You know, I never saw who knocked me out." Just a hint of an accusation tinged my voice.

His eyes flared with gold. "What are you implying?"

"It's just interesting that my injuries mean that you have to keep the curse, just like the Heavenly Host would want, and we can't go after Adonis." I'd planned to play it cool, but in the dead of night, with the pain wracking my body, I was kind of failing at that.

"If you want to pull the curse from me now instead of in the morning, be my guest."

I gritted my teeth, forcing myself to sit up as agony danced up my spine. "It doesn't hurt that much," I said defensively.

Kratos touched his heart—maybe unconsciously reminded of his own pain. His heart hurt when he didn't hunt humans like he was supposed to.

If I took his curse away, all that would change.

"How does this work, exactly?" he asked.

"I just need to see the curse around your throat. It looks like black vines. Then, I'll pull them from you."

He arched his neck, and I let my eyes linger over his throat. The stones in my forehead began to warm up, and I stared as the ropes of dark, thorny magic began to writhe around his skin. The invasive magic of the heavens.

Instinctively, I reached for them. I stroked the magic vines with the tip of my finger, scraping it across the thorns. Blue light beamed from my fingertips. At the touch, a powerful jolt of ecstasy raced through my hand, arcing up my arm and blazing into my chest.

I gasped, my back arching as euphoria surged. This magic wasn't splitting my body apart. Instead, it was doing something entirely different and somewhat mortifying to my body. There was something sexual about this magic, and my body warmed, thighs clenching under the sheets.

My eyes opened. I stared at Kratos's neck, watching the seal dissipate like dark smoke. I was panting, a thin sheen of sweat on my body.

Kratos's body had gone rigid, his back arched, and golden light radiated from his chest. His fiery gaze met mine, and I tried to ignore what this meant—Kratos could now bone with impunity.

He closed his eyes again, as if in prayer. "Your magic fingertips have stroked me to perfection."

"You're doing that on purpose, aren't you?"

He didn't answer, seemingly lost in his own thoughts. His eyes were still closed, hand on his heart—the very part of his body that had tormented him for a thousand years.

After a few moments, he met my gaze again with a reverent look. "Free," he said quietly. He looked down at his chest, his brow furrowed. "After a thousand years, I control my fate now. I will kill only when I want to. The things that I've done...."

His voice trailed off.

I almost felt bad for the guy. Unless he had betrayed us, and then I wanted him to die a painful death.

"It's over now," I said quietly. "You're free. Like you said."

The back of my neck throbbed, and I rubbed it. The blast of magic from the Old Gods had dulled some of my pain, but it hadn't healed me completely. Only Adonis seemed to have that power.

I studied Kratos closely. Maybe he'd wanted the curse pulled from him, but I still didn't trust him.

"How much time?" I asked.

"Till what?"

"How much time do you think we have until we all die?"

"That's anyone's guess. None of us knows what the Heavenly Host are doing, or where they are."

"Well, someone is going to have to find out."

5

Three days. That was all it had taken for me to heal —at least enough so that I could haul my broken ass out of bed. My ribs and shoulder still hurt like hell, but I could put one foot in front of another.

I might have the power of the Old Gods, but I wasn't immortal. The fae had long lives, but we were still mortal creatures. And damned if I hadn't felt that mortality when the iron arrows had slammed into me. Still, I was pretty sure the gemstones were helping me recover faster.

Last night, Drakon had arrived at Hotemet, carrying a piece of stone Kratos had identified. A sand-colored chunk of Sadeckrav Castle.

Assuming we could trust this form of primitive communication, we needed to take a little trip across the English Channel. It seemed Adonis was in the torture palace, just like I'd feared. But I needed a plan before I rushed over the English Channel to France. I didn't want to screw up this rescue.

With the morning sun filtering through the leaves, I followed the winding path through the forest, moving as quickly as my battered body would take me. I hadn't seen a single sentinel out here this morning. Had they deserted Kratos since I removed the curse from his neck, ripping away his apocalyptic seal? Whatever the case, it definitely made it easier to move around without them.

My feet crunched over the leaves, and the crisp February air felt cool against my skin. That morning, I'd summoned Yasmin through a few flicks of the candle in the bathroom mirror. I hadn't spoken to her in weeks, but if anyone could help me develop a plan to rescue Adonis, it was her.

As I walked, I closed my eyes. I tried to block out the rising panic—that little, niggling fear that the Heavenly Host would murder the world's entire population at any moment. I tried to tune out the dark visions of the torments Adonis might be enduring. Panic was the enemy of strategy.

I breathed in the scent of oaks. As I did, my mind flooded again with images of Eden—grape vines curling up a fig tree, a gleaming blue river winding between thorny shrubs—a crooked cottage, where Adonis sat by a roaring fireplace....

I opened my eyes, stunned for a moment to find this vision alive around me—the fig trees standing where oaks had been, purple thistle instead of deadfall, a rushing azure river. A cottage stood among the trees.

Holy shit. The gemstones seemed to have intensified my powers of glamouring. I'd created the illusion of Paradise. As I stared at the vision around me, euphoria rippled over my body.

I blinked, and the illusion disappeared before my eyes. I hadn't even realized it was possible to glamour the world around me. I'd glamoured other people before—sentient beings. Never objects, and definitely not an entire landscape.

I stared down at my fingertips. So, I could now create an illusion out of thin air. I concentrated on the space above my fingertips, trying to conjure the illusion of a butterfly. Warm magic flickered over my forehead, tingling along my arms. For just a moment, something winged and pumpkin-orange burst into the air, before the illusion shattered.

I clenched my fists, no longer sure if I was creating illusions or just straight up hallucinating.

I bit my lip, remembering what I'd seen that morning. When I'd woken, light was streaming through the windows—and along with it, the vines from outside the castle had worked their way into the room, snaking over the floor toward my bed. I kept feeling as if the forest were straining for me.

Unless, of course, I was just losing my mind. Maybe a fae like me was never meant for this godlike power. Maybe it would make me insane.

I hugged myself, walking along the winding path again. As I moved deeper into the woods, my thoughts kept returning to that perfect Garden of Eden, and I was sure I could hear the song of the Old Gods whispering through the back of my mind.

"Eden..." I whispered to myself. "The perfect paradise."

I clenched my fists until my fingernails bit into my palms. You know what else was the enemy of strategy? Fantasizing about damn gardens. *Stay focused, Ruby.*

When I reached the grove of mulberry trees—overgrown with hellebore and cockle weeds—I knew I was nearly at the meeting spot. And when I spotted the mouth of the pine-flanked cave that was our meeting point, I sped up my pace. Yasmin and I had to make a plan, *stat*.

I crossed into the dank cavern, where I found her—the Queen of Poisons.

Yasmin's dark eyes were wide in the dim light. "Well, well. It's been a while, Agent Hudole." She stared at the stones in my forehead. "What in the gods' names are those things in your head?"

I touched them gently. "Yeah. I guess we didn't get to update you about this yet. I stole these from one of the Old Gods, who I found in a cave in Lebanon when I was trying to raise one of the horsemen from the dead. And now they're in my forehead, and I think they might be messing with my thoughts a little."

Her eyes widened. "You did *what?*"

"I accidentally raised the horsemen from the dead after stealing gemstones from the gods," I repeated, trying to act blasé. "I think you'll agree this situation could have happened to anyone."

Something like rage tightened her features. "Slow down. The horsemen were dead? And you brought them back?"

How did I explain to her that I couldn't just let Adonis die, that if she knew him like I did, she'd save him, too?

I traced my fingertips across the gemstones. "Look, the horsemen are at war with each other, and Adonis might be our only hope. Problem is, he's been abducted, and now the odds are against us. He and I were ambushed, and I'm going to need your help to get him back." My gaze flicked to the skies. "Look, we don't have a ton of time. The Heavenly Host are somewhere on earth, and we're all gonna die, like, any second, so...."

"You want to save the Horseman of Death. I'm not even sure what to say to you."

I let out a sigh. This was a hard sell, and I hadn't prepared well enough. "Adonis has been working against the other horsemen. His seal was never broken, and his curse never took hold. For thousands of years, he staved off the power of the curse by hurting himself. With the magic of the Old Gods, I was able to pull it from him. We *need* him to fight the other angels, or we don't stand a chance. The Heavenly Host are mortal on earth. Once we know where they are, he can kill them all in an instant."

"And what makes you think he would do that?"

"He's the one who helped me get the stones. He sacrificed his life so I could rid the earth of the horsemen. He's only here because I brought him back."

From there, we stood there in the cave for what seemed an eternity, arguing over Adonis until she reluctantly conceded I might have a point, that he *might* be a key to our survival.

"Maybe I will keep an open mind." Yasmin's dark eyes were fixed on me intently. "But don't rule anyone out as a leak. Hazel, Kratos, the fae boy—they're all suspects. Feed them false information, and see what they do with it. Find out which of them passes it on to the other angels. If you allow them to keep passing on information, we don't have a chance in hell of defeating the destructive angels."

"Like leaking a fake plan of attack?"

She shrugged. "That could work. Get your enemy to show up to a specific location. You'll know who leaked the information when you know where they show up."

Seemed simple enough. "Maybe I can do this at the same time I'm rescuing Adonis."

Yasmin crossed her arms. "When you go to Sadeckrav, I'm going with you. There's no way I'm letting you make decisions on your own at this point. Not with the stakes this high. I just need to find someone to look after my daughter, and we'll head off together. I want to make sure you don't cock it up this time."

I raised my eyebrows, not entirely sure I liked her tone. "You've lost a bit of faith in me, haven't you?"

"Like you said, we don't have time to mess around. The Heavenly Host have come to earth, and it's only a matter of time before they slaughter each and every one of us. And apart from your terrible decision-making, I'm not sure you're handling your new powers well."

"What makes you say that?"

"I saw you muttering to yourself as you approached me."

I crossed my arms. Okay, maybe I was losing my mind. "Right, come with me if you want. But what's important is that I want to get back to Adonis as soon as we can."

"Don't rule out Adonis as the traitor, either."

"What? No. He was captured, along with an asshole angel named Muriel."

She shrugged. "It could have been a ruse on his part. Maybe he and Muriel were in on it. What if you were the real target, and the plan simply failed?"

My throat tightened at the idea. I didn't want to argue the point too much. It would just make me seem biased. "Fine. Maybe it was Adonis. Any chance you have any good news to share? I could really use some right now."

"Perhaps. While the angels have been fighting amongst themselves, things have changed in the human cities. Humans have been organizing themselves into armies. They've formed a resistance. Your former rookery in Whitechapel is one of the command centers. While the Hunter no longer patrols the streets, they want to take the opportunity to rise up against the angels."

My eyebrows shot up. I'd been desperate to know what happened to Alex and my other rookery-mates. "Do you know who's involved?"

Yasmin nodded. "I've identified the leaders, but they don't trust the Institute. I'm working on making inroads."

I took a deep breath. "That Whitechapel rookery you mentioned."

"Yeah?"

"If you can find a man named Alex living among the resistance, I want to know how he's doing. And his friends, too." Adonis had taken them to a safe house out of the city after

Johnny had nearly killed them, but it was possible they'd found their way back.

"I'll find out what I can, but they don't trust outsiders like me. The Institute has a bad reputation since we barred the Tower doors to most of London's population. Plus, people are more spooked than ever in the past few weeks."

I frowned. "Now? Why now? The Hunter is gone."

"People are afraid of what they don't understand. And right now, there's a new puzzle haunting London's streets."

"What's that?"

"Humans are dying, just like they have been for over a year now. Starvation, disease. Except now, their bodies are going missing. They're buried and dug up again. And no one knows why."

A cold shiver rippled over my spine. I had no idea what that meant, either, but it didn't sound wonderful. If I had to guess, humans might be eating the dead, and I was superstitious enough to believe that was a line that should never be crossed without inviting the wrath of the gods.

❦ 6 ❦

Moonlight washed over the darkened landscape. I stood before the window of my room, staring at an unlit candle.

To an outside observer, it may not have seemed the best use of time given our current, desperate situation, but I needed to test my new powers to see if I could use them. I wanted to create the illusion of a flame. I squinted my eyes, failing to spark anything before me.

A cool breeze filtered in through the open windows, rippling over my silk dress and raising goosebumps on my skin. The wild symphony of the Old Gods sang in the back of my mind.

I closed my eyes, imagining a flame dancing at the tip of the wick. When I opened them again, a spark of light burst into the air before dying out again.

Almost.

I still had time to work on this skill—assuming it had been real.

But right now, I had to speak to Hazel.

I pulled open the door, crossing into the hallway. I had a

good idea where I could find my sister. As much as I'd tried to keep her away from the bar, it had become her favorite haunt.

I hated the idea of lying to Hazel, but I supposed Yasmin was right. I had to suspect everyone.

As expected, I found her sitting in the bar's shadows, nursing a bright blue cocktail by herself. She leaned back in her wooden bench, raising her glass. "Sister. You look better."

"Well, I was in bed for three days." I frowned at her cocktail. "Are you just helping yourself in here?"

She took a sip of the disturbingly fluorescent drink, ignoring my question. "Since you've recovered, does that mean we're going after Adonis?"

"I have a plan. But I'll need your reptilian friend to give us a ride to Sadeckrav Castle."

And here was the lie. A lie was no different to any other performance, right? *Put on a good show, Ruby.*

"And then what?" she asked.

"You can't tell *anyone* this. But Yasmin is connecting us with a demonic assassin named Balam. He's going to arrive, cloaked in darkness, at the Porte de Richelieu at the Louvre. He'll slaughter everyone in his path until he gets to Adonis."

"Just one demon?" she asked.

"He's a legendary assassin. That's all it will take."

"What kind of demon?"

She was asking for an awful lot of details, here. "An alû demon. He'll be completely stealthy."

"Interesting." She lifted her cocktail glass. "You want to stay for a drink? I call this the Apocalyptic Julep. It's three parts whiskey, one part vodka, some of the blue alcohol, and some other number of parts of that green stuff."

I gagged. "Midori?"

"I guess. What the fuck is a julep, anyway?"

"Not *that*." I rose. As soon as I got the chance, I was

going to throw all this alcohol away. But first—I had to move on to my second lie. "I can't stay for a drink. I need to get ready for our trip. Find Uthyr, and let him know we need to get to France."

I FOUND ELAN IN THE KITCHENS, ROLLING OUT PASTRY dough on the countertop. Flour covered his sweatshirt, which featured a cartoon cat hanging from a tree and the words *Hang in There!*

Really, there was no way in hell Elan was a double agent, but I had to dot all my i's and cross all my t's.

A steaming Cornish pasty lay on the table, and my mouth watered. "Mind if I grab this?"

"Go for it." Elan's cheeks had their characteristic ruddy glow.

I bit into the rich beef and potato filling. *For the love of the gods, we can't lose Elan.*

"I need your help, Elan."

Shock lit up his features. "Mine?"

I nodded. "I want to get Adonis back from Sadeckrav Castle, and I'm gonna need a team."

"You want me to be part of your team?"

"I need people I can trust." I glanced furtively around me. "The truth is, I don't trust Kratos, and I want someone to keep an eye on him. Do you think you can do that?"

"Of course."

And here comes my next lie.

"Good. We're taking a flight on Uthyr tomorrow. Yasmin has hooked us up with a legendary shadow demon assassin. He'll be glamoured as an angel guard, and he'll waltz right into Aereus's main entrance." I bit my lip. "Just please don't tell anyone else of the plan. Not even Hazel or Kratos. I'm not sure I can trust them."

He smiled, his cheeks dimpling. "I'm honored to be part of your team."

BEFORE I EVEN GOT TO THE CELESTIAL ROOM IN THE Tower of Silence, the rich smell of cedar wafted through the halls, curling around my body. Goosebumps rose on my skin, and I wasn't sure if it was from the drafty castle air that skimmed over my silky dress, or the raw power I often felt emanating from Kratos whenever I got anywhere near him.

On the top floor of the Tower of Silence, two armored guards stood before a heavy wooden door. Without a word, they shifted aside, and the doors swung open.

Under a large glass dome, Kratos moved over the floor, carving his sword through the air. He was shirtless, and silver light washed over his chiseled muscles. A faint sheen of sweat covered his body, and he seemed to be fighting invisible attackers with a level of viciousness usually reserved for virgin night at the vampire ball.

Unless he lost his mind completely, I had a feeling that once he finally found his way out of his castle, the man would have no problems finding someone to stroke him to perfection.

Perfection ... a perfect paradise....

For a moment, the hollows of my mind flashed with vivid images—a cottage in a garden by a river's edge, the leaves outside tinged with autumn gold. Adonis, sat at table before a roaring fire, with a bowl of soup in his lap.

Paradise.

Distracted, I stumbled. My phantom life—the one with the cottage and the soup—had somehow seemed more real than what was actually going on now. I blinked, and it took me a moment to realize I was still in the Celestial Room, with a shirtless horseman of the apocalypse. These gemstones were really fucking with me.

Kratos stared at me, lowering his sword. His body looked rigid with tension. "Are you all right?"

I clenched my jaw. "Yes, why?"

"You don't seem yourself." He lifted his sword again for another brutal slash through the air.

"Neither do you. Working off a little tension, are we?"

Slash. "I have a lot on my mind right now. What's your excuse?"

I brushed my fingertips over the gemstones in my forehead. "Just getting used to my new powers, I think. They can overwhelm my thoughts." I wasn't about to tell him about my new ability to conjure illusions out of thin air, but it was obvious something had changed about me. "I have to resist their influence, I think."

In fact, I had to resist my own intense fantasies.

He lowered his sword, but his knuckles had gone white on the hilt. "Resisting urges is something that I understand well."

True—a thousand years of abstinence couldn't have been easy. "How did you manage it?"

He closed the distance between us, his golden eyes piercing in the darkness. "When the temptations of the flesh began to lure me in, when a beautiful woman's body and her scent drew me closer, I would remember my mother's death. It killed my ardor."

It *did* sound like a mood killer. "What happened to your mother?"

"She was a Viking warrior. A shield maiden. She was captured during a raid in Britain and burned to death for witchcraft. I was only eleven. It wasn't a fast death, either."

His eyes took on a faraway look. "But her dreams for me were clear—that I fulfill my destiny when the time came." He met my eyes again, his gaze sharpening. "I'm afraid I would have disappointed her."

I didn't say what I was really thinking—that it was a cruel thing for her to ask, and she sounded like a shitty mother.

He closed his eyes, running his hand over his heart. "When I thought I might give in to the temptations of the flesh, I thought of her dying body. I thought of the curse that the Heavenly Host placed on humans—the curse of anticipating mortality. My mother knew she was going to die, and thinking of that killed my cravings."

So Kratos could be a bit of a downer. And clearly, he was having something of a hard time adjusting to his new, curse-less life. Was he regretting it?

I cocked my head. "And after all those years resisting temptations, what made you change your mind? Why did you want the curse removed?"

"Because I never asked for this. My destiny will be my choice. I am Conquest, and I control my fate. Not the memory of my mother. Not the Heavenly Host. No one but me."

Reasonable. Unfortunately, I wasn't sure his method would work for me. If I summoned my worst memories, they'd drive me insane: my mother's torn arm after I'd savaged her in one of my feral states; Marcus being slaughtered before my eyes; Adonis, after I'd killed him. I was already fighting madness as it was.

He looked me over slowly. "You've made a rather amazing recovery."

"I have. And I'm ready to go after Adonis now."

Slash. "I haven't come up with a plan yet. Like I said. I've been distracted."

And also, you don't really care that much if Adonis is tortured within an inch of his life. "What if I have a plan?"

Slash. "You? What's your plan?"

"The Institute is on our side. I've met with one of their agents. She's offered sending us an assassin, who I will glamour as a cherub. He's going to sneak right in to the Porte des Lions entrance. Just—don't tell anyone else. I'm not sure I can trust anyone. Not even Hazel."

He pivoted, his sword carving a ferocious arc. "And when do you plan to travel?"

"Tomorrow. I want you to come."

"Fine." A hint of anger laced his tone.

The stones in my forehead began to heat up. *Rid the earth of the angels...*

I clamped down on the voice in my mind, but the sentiment remained. If Kratos betrayed us, I would use my new powers to end him, fast.

7

I wrapped my arms tightly around Kratos's neck, while strands of my red hair whipped in front of my eyes. As we soared over the English Channel, the briny scent of the sea whispered through the air. I carried my bow and arrow on my back, and a poison-tipped knife at my belt. I hardly went anywhere without my weapons these days.

Just above our flight path, Uthyr carried Elan, Yasmin, and Hazel on his back.

Yasmin had insisted that everyone come. If we found out one of them was a traitor, she wanted them dealt with. Fast.

Except—no matter what Hazel might have done, I wouldn't let anyone touch her.

Exhausted, I blinked my eyes, fighting to stay awake. Last night, I'd spent hours in one of Kratos's libraries with the curtains closed. I'd needed time to practice my new illusion-conjuring skills. Instead of sleeping, I'd managed to summon a menagerie of creatures inspired by the medieval books and tapestries I'd found: cats with weirdly human faces, men with arrows up their butts, medieval rabbits who stood on their hind legs and wielded swords, knights fighting giant snails....

I'd learned two things. One, medieval artists were into some weird shit.

And two, the key to creating illusions was to turn off my thoughts. I had to summon the images vividly in my mind's eye. Then, they'd simply appear around me. But if any amount of chatter started flowing in my mind, it ruined the whole thing. The illusion would pop like a bubble before me. Basically, I had to get all Zen.

After a night of practice, I was *pretty* sure I'd be able to summon the illusions I needed.

"Can you glamour all of us?" Kratos's voice was low in my ear. "At least make us less noticeable?"

I nodded. It was time to go into stealth mode. I closed my eyes, summoning a glamour of unobtrusiveness.

By the time we reached Paris, it felt like we'd been flying for days. In synch with the dragon, we swooped lower over the city.

I gazed below at an encampment in one of Paris's parks. Tangerine rays of light slanted over a park dotted with tents and fire pits. Small gardens for growing food spread below me, and children wandered among them. I watched a dark-haired toddler sitting by his mother stuff his face with what might be mashed potatoes. Here, even among all the death of the Great Nightmare, life was thriving. And if we didn't stop the horsemen, all this would turn to ash.

WE STOOD IN THE JARDIN DES TUILERIES AMONG THE DEAD trees, staring at the Louvre. Outside the main entrances to the old palace, a few cherubs milled around with angelic soldiers.

Now, all I had to do was create my illusions and find out if one of my team had passed on the information to Aereus.

I met Yasmin's gaze, and she nodded curtly. She was the only one here I hadn't lied to, the only one who actually knew what was about to happen.

I stared at the palace before us—the pale golden stone, ruddied by the setting sun. *Adonis, I'm coming for you.*

What had Aereus done to him in his palace? I couldn't think about the torture garden, the Catherine wheel—

Stop.

I swallowed hard. I needed my mind to go quiet if I was going to get this to work.

Hazel nudged me. "Where is the assassin?" she whispered.

I shot her a fierce look. "Shhhh."

Adonis, are you here? I felt a warm, tingling tug on my shoulder—the exact place where Adonis had marked me. He was here. Even if I couldn't hear him now, I could feel him.

Let your mind go quiet, Ruby.

I took a deep breath, focusing on stilling the chatter in my brain. I closed my eyes, imagining Eden before the fall—before language ruined everything for everyone.

Sunlight streamed through the fig trees, and a deep blue river rushed through it all. My back arched as my body surged with a power older than words. *Paradise.*

And in my mind's eye, I conjured the three assassins—a wisp of darkness at the Porte de Richelieu for Hazel, a cherub at the Porte des Lions for Kratos. And for Elan, an angelic soldier marching for the main entrance.

I opened my eyes again and smiled as I watched my creations crossing the stone piazza. Slowly, I scanned the others in my group—each of them watching the entrance I'd told them about.

As my glamour worked, my body surged with a song of ancient magic, my skin tingling. I stared as one of the entrances burst open, giving away our informant. Dozens of angels streamed out, swords drawn, to surround my illusion, and shock slammed into me.

They'd been expecting him. I made him turn and run, sprinting away from them, and they followed the illusion in hot pursuit. A stream of angel soldiers rushed out of the Louvre, following him.

And now I knew that Elan was our traitor. Rage ignited in my mind, and I whirled on him, teeth bared.

"What in the gods' names is going on?" asked Kratos.

I could feel myself going feral, about to rip Elan to pieces. "What's going on," I said, "is that I was testing you all to see who was leaking info. And Elan is the one feeding information to the other horsemen. Isn't that right, Elan?"

I felt a sharp shove from the side. "You were testing me, too?" said Hazel. "Asshole. You should have known better."

Elan stumbled back, trembling in his cat sweater, his eyes wide. I *nearly* felt sorry for him—apart from the fact that he was responsible for Adonis's capture.

"So, Elan—"

Before I could finish my sentence, Kratos rushed for him, lifting the wiry fae by his neck. "Explain yourself, fae."

Elan emitted only a choking sound, his face turning red.

"He can't speak while you're strangling him," I pointed out.

Kratos let him drop to the ground, and Elan looked up at Kratos, his entire body shaking.

"Adonis always hated me," Elan stammered, meeting my gaze. "He hates the fae. He'll always hate the fae. Don't you realize that? He thinks we're animals. He'll never—"

I hardly even saw the gesture Kratos made—just a subtle flick of his wrist was all it took to sever Elan's head from his body.

I grimaced at the sight of his body collapsing to the stones, blood pooling around him.

Kratos turned back to me. "I thought we'd heard enough."

Hazel crossed her arms. "Okay, jerk. Now you know who the leak was, and that it wasn't me, which you should have already known. So what's the actual plan?"

Sunlight glinted off Kratos's armor. "You're the Bringer of Light. You're supposed to be able to defeat the Heavenly Host. You blocked them from the earth one time. Can't you do it again?"

I shook my head. Not without dying, so ... I was holding off on that for now. "In theory, yes. Except—every time I try to use powerful magic, I go feral. I lose control, forget what I'm doing. My teeth come out. The Old Gods take over my mind completely, and I can't control the magic."

Kratos looked unimpressed. "I think I can manage you, Ruby. You need to at least try."

I didn't want to explain all of it. That if I used the magic of the Old Gods to its full extent, it would kill me. News like that would just extinguish all hope.

But maybe it was worth one more shot.

I swallowed hard. "Okay, here goes. If I start to lose my shit, pain can snap me out of it." I closed my eyes, tuning in to the faint sound of the Old Gods' song. I felt the gemstones in my forehead warm up, and ancient magic vibrated over my body.

My mind flashed with images—the Garden of Eden, feet sinking into the dirt, vines curving around naked flesh. My canines began to lengthen, yearning for blood. Angelic blood.

Kill the angels....

A peaty haze clouded my mind, and I whirled, my gaze landing on the copper one. *A bringer of death should not walk the earth....*

My nostrils flared, my body begging to explode with light. The power of the Old Gods was going to rip me apart, and I craved life.

In the next heartbeat, my canines were at Kratos's throat, piercing flesh, the sweet rush of blood—

A sharp smack to the side of my head snapped me out of it. Delicious angel blood dripped from my lips, and I wiped the back of my hand over my mouth.

My body was shaking. Yep, the Old Gods wanted the angels dead, but they wanted me dead, too. Probably because I'd stolen the gemstones from them in the first place. "Sorry. I'm afraid I still need to refine this a bit."

Kratos had clamped his fingers over his neck wound. "Interesting. The Bringer of Light has a bit of a biting problem."

Yasmin stepped forward, the wind toying with her hair. "It's fine. We have a plan B that may at least buy us some time. Ruby needs to create a serious decoy, so we can sneak in another entrance." Her dark eyebrows drew together. "How many demon soldiers can you conjure at once?"

"As many as we want. I just need to let my mind go blank."

"Shouldn't be hard," Hazel grumbled. "Since you've got literal rocks in your head."

"I get it. You're mad at me. Let's move on." I focused on Kratos. "You've been here before. Once we get inside, any idea where we need to go? The torture garden? A dungeon, maybe?"

"Aereus created a dungeon in the lower level," said Kratos. "It's protected by wraithlike creatures called the *dames blanches*. We'll need to be very careful with them."

I blinked, mentally translating. "The white ladies?"

"What are they going to do?" asked Hazel. "Throw pumpkin spice lattes at us? Strangle us with yoga pants?"

"Are they going to make us listen to Taylor Swift?" I knew this was serious, but I couldn't stop myself.

"They're more dangerous than they sound." Kratos looked

annoyed. "They're part fae, part phantom, and they can drive a person mad."

"How do we defeat them?" I asked.

"I have no idea," Kratos said. "But I can tell you that when we go in there, we're going to create chaos. If we get separated, we'll meet back here."

A tug pulled at my shoulder—the mark from Adonis. I brushed my fingers over the spot, the theta Adonis had marked me with. "I can feel him here. He's pulling me toward him. I might be able to use our link to find him. Hang on."

I turned to my companions, inspecting the glamour. I'd already shielded us with a glamour of unobtrusiveness, but it wasn't foolproof. They were still visible if you knew where to look.

"I'm making us into angels before we go in there." I closed my eyes, summoning my magic. The glamour tingled down the length of my arm, and when I opened my eyes again, I was standing with three other winged, white-clad angels.

I breathed in deeply. "Okay. Let me focus. When I say 'go,' we run for the Porte de Richelieu." I closed my eyes, tuning in to the subtle feel of the breeze on my skin, the gentle, cool mist dotting my face. My skin buzzed and hummed with the magic of the Old Gods.

I turned down the chatter in my mind, summoning a vision of a wispy, black smoke that writhed and curled before the glass pyramid in the piazza.

Then, from within the dark tendrils of smoke, a demonic horde began to emerge, as if slipping through a wormhole. Horns, armor, black eyes, and shadowy magic whipping around their bodies, slashing through the air. Even though I knew they weren't real, a chill rippled up my spine at the sight of them.

The doors to the main entrance slammed open, and

angels streamed out to fight their illusory enemy. I stroked the strap over my chest, my bow bringing me comfort. I had a feeling I'd be using it soon.

"Now!" I said.

In our angelic disguises, we broke into a run across the piazza.

8

At any moment, the angelic hordes would realize they were fighting phantoms, and they'd be scanning the palace for invaders.

"We have to move quickly," I rasped as I ran.

We'd slipped through the Porte de Richelieu unnoticed, our feet pounding the floor as we raced through the marble palace halls. Chaos whirled around us, a river of angels flowing through the halls toward the main entrance, where my phantom demons attacked.

As we moved, I felt the tug on my shoulder, a sort of certainty that spurred me onward. The theta linked me to Adonis, guiding me through the palace.

"Left," I called out.

Fleeing through the marble halls, I felt the inexorable pull to Adonis, as if his dark magic had coiled itself around my collarbone. I just had to follow his lead.

We moved swiftly through a hall of medieval Catholic art —the walls lined with statues of saints and ancient wooden confessional booths.

We raced down a marble stairwell, moving into the medieval foundations. Lantern light flickered over rough sandstone.

Even from here, I could hear the shouts of the angels as they streamed back into the Louvre, looking for their real attackers. Right now, the only thing keeping us from their notice was our angelic glamour.

Almost there, Adonis. On the lower level, I could feel his magic even more powerfully. In this ancient part of the palace, our footfalls echoed off the stone ceilings, and we kicked up dust as we ran.

But as we rounded a corner though the tunnels, a sharp, searing pain bit into my skin—my arms, my neck and face. I ground to a halt, and my own screams echoed off the halls, mingling with Hazel's and Yasmin's.

"What's wrong with you?" barked Kratos. "Stop screaming."

Whatever it was, he was fine.

I stared down at my arms, watching the glamour shimmer away until only my own clothing remained, coated in deep gray powder. My heart leapt into my throat.

"Iron dust!" I shouted. It was burning away the magical glamour with a startling pain. As an angel, only Kratos was unaffected.

My heart slammed against my ribs. Now, nothing shielded us from Aereus and his angelic horde if they should happen to search the lower levels. We were exposed.

"We have to keep moving," said Yasmin.

Kratos began to chant in Angelic, to try to draw the iron off our bodies, but more of it kept pouring from the ceilings.

As his Angelic words echoed around us, wispy white creatures crept out of the stones—gaunt women with long, white hair and haunted green eyes. They smelled of ancient riverbeds, like damp sediment and algae. Their appearance sent a tendril of fear coiling through my gut.

One look into their oily eyes rooted me in place. Now, even Kratos had frozen. My pulse raced out of control. What would Aereus do to us if he found us here? We'd be ripped to shreds in his torture garden—slowly. Perhaps over a period of centuries. Adonis would remain imprisoned forever. Oh, and the rest of the earth would die. Not ideal, really.

Still, the *dames blanches* transfixed me.

Fuck. Balls. We need to keep going.

My heart jumped into my throat as one of them crept near me, slipping her arm around my body. They looked like wraiths, but the touch of her tangible flesh against my skin told me they weren't. This woman was as solid as I was, and a stroke of her cold fingertips against the back of my neck sent an icy lick of fear racing up my spine. She hissed as she touched me, as though the contact pained her, and yet she didn't stop.

My mind whirled with brutal images of Aereus and his Catherine wheel—his sharp, iron instruments that could tear flesh from bone. Right now, it was looking like that was my future. My knees were going weak with fear.

The *dame blanche* muffled my mouth with her hand, suffocating the air out of my lungs.

Her damp touch felt strangely tempting—an escape from the fear. It was like she was luring me toward death, until I wanted to give in to her embrace. *La belle dame sans merci.* I wanted her to drag me under the water, deep below an icy surface where silence reigned. Where Aereus could never find me. A dark, angel-less place, a primordial home.

I clamped my eyes shut, desperate to stay in control of myself. *We're running out of time. Running out of time to get Adonis, to save ourselves from a horrendous fate.*

The *dame blanche*'s arms slid around me more tightly, the embrace of a desperate lover. If I gave in to her....

Distantly, I heard the shouts of angels echoing from the stairwell above us. They were coming for us. My heart slammed hard against my ribs.

Move. Now.

What had Kratos told me about mastering my impulses? He dwelled in his darkest memories. I needed to do that now, to get us out of here before it was too late.

In my mind's eye, I summoned the vision of dragons ripping Hazel from the earth, of the dragon who slaughtered Marcus, his body turning to ash on the pavement—

Grief pierced my chest, ripping me from the watery allure of the *dame blanche*. I slammed my elbows into her, knocking her away from me, and she fell backward.

Around me, the *dames blanches* writhed around the bodies of my companions, feeding from them.

The pain of iron still seared my skin. Hadn't Kratos said the *dames* were fae, also? That's why she had hissed when she touched me; the iron burned her skin, too.

I growled, my canines lengthening as I whirled on my attacker. A phantom breeze toyed with her white hair, and she let out a low, eerie wail as she glared at me.

Battle fury arced through my veins. As quick as a storm wind, I scooped iron dust off the floor and rushed for the *dame blanche*.

When she opened her lips to howl again, I shoved the iron into her mouth. She gagged, choking on it until her body began to hiss, steam rising from her flesh. She crumpled to the floor.

I whirled to survey the others. Kratos had just managed to free himself, and he swung his sword through one of the *dames*. She leapt away from him, and his blade *whooshed* harmlessly through the air.

"The dust!" I screamed. "The iron dust."

He caught my eye, and understanding sparked in his gaze. In the next moment, his Angelic words were clattering around us, reverberating in my skull like curses. Iron dust whirled into the air, swooping around the *dames blanches* and coating their ethereal skin. Agonized howls rose from their throats. As the dust covered them, a sound like a gale through a window crack whistled around us, and the *dames blanches* evaporated before our eyes. At last, nothing remained of them but a few wisps of steam and the dank scent of a riverbed.

I nodded at Kratos. "Nicely done. Now let's get the fuck out of here, because the Host is coming for us."

I broke into a sprint again, looking over my shoulder as I ran. Already, I could hear the sounds of Aereus's army reverberating off the ancient stone walls, just behind us. I pumped my arms faster, desperate to find my way to Adonis before we were captured.

I felt a slight sense of relief when Kratos began chanting in Angelic—I had no idea what the words meant, but hopefully he could stave off the oncoming horde for a bit.

The tug in my shoulder intensified. As we moved deeper into the dungeons, I felt an overwhelming need to wrap my arms around Adonis, to breathe in the intoxicating scent of myrrh.

But quickly, that desire was replaced by a fiery rage. And that meant Aereus was near, getting closer. He was stoking my bloodlust to a fever pitch. In my mind's eye, an image arose—Aereus capturing us, strapping Hazel and me to one of his iron contraptions, spikes tearing at our flesh. White-hot fury ripped my mind apart, so intense my body shook uncontrollably.

Shouts rang out behind us, and an arrow whistled past my ear. Then, another.

"I can't hold them off any longer," said Kratos.

"Ruby!" Yasmin shouted. "Your magic."

I want to destroy him. I pivoted, facing the oncoming horde —my heart about to explode. Aereus was leading the charge.

The stones in my forehead blazed, a wild power ripping me apart. My canines lengthened, and a growl tore from my throat. As magic exploded from my body, images flooded my mind—a garden paradise. And me, running wild and naked alongside a river—hunting an angel. The enemy. I captured him, claws digging into his perfect skin, teeth tearing at his flesh in an orgy of blood. Ecstasy coursed through me. I'd been born to kill him. The beast taking down the angel, the way it was always meant to be.

Except, the symphony of the Old Gods crested around me. Cracks formed in my body, light beaming from them. The power of the Old Gods was going to rip me apart, tear through me like teeth through flesh.

Smack. I landed hard on the stone floor, my entire body shaking wildly. I rolled over to see Kratos staring down at me.

"You were frothing at the mouth. But you managed to make a shield."

My canines had pierced my lower lip, and I tasted salty blood. Apparently, I could always count on Kratos to smack me upside the head when I needed it.

Just to my left blazed a shield of pearly white light—with the angelic horde trapped on the other side. Somehow, without even realizing what I was doing, I'd managed to create a blockade. On the other side, fire burned in Aereus's eyes.

Slowly, I pushed myself to my feet.

Aereus pulled his sword from his scabbard. He was screaming—probably in Angelic—but the shield had silenced him.

Kratos was shouting back at him in Angelic, the words clamoring in my mind.

The Horseman of War slammed his sword against the shield. *Thunk*. It sounded like metal slamming against metal. *Thunk*.

The faintest of fractures appeared in the shield. We were still running on borrowed time.

❦ 9 ❦

Hazel tugged my arm. "We need to keep going before he breaks through that thing."

Aereus's sword *thunked* behind us, and we took off running again.

My body was still shaking from the magical burst. I didn't want to think too long about that image in my mind—the one of me ripping apart an angel's flesh. The gray eyes—had they been Adonis's? I couldn't escape the sense that I was fated to kill him—the beast taking down the angel, destroying his otherworldly perfection. Was that my destiny?

Thunk.

I had no time to figure that out now, not when Aereus was hot on our heels.

When we rounded the next corner in the stone hall, we found a row of angelic guards standing before a dark hall. I nocked two arrows, letting them fly straight into two angels' hearts. Kratos flicked his wrist, and the other three fell to their knees before him. One by one, they pulled knives from their belts and plunged them into their own guts.

Kratos was starting to impress me more and more by the minute.

A dark, barren hall loomed in front of us, and a silence fell over us, heavy as damp earth.

Tension rippled over my skin as we moved through the dim hall. Empty cells, barred with iron, lined either side of us.

Thunk. Thunk. Distantly, the sound of sword hitting shield echoed around us, spurring me on.

A sense of panic was starting to climb up my throat. Was Adonis here at all? I'd been following a tug in my shoulder, and it was entirely possible I'd been imagining it.

"Adonis!" I shouted, fear tightening my chest.

A flash of white in the corner of my eye halted me in my tracks.

Thunk. Thunk.

I whirled to find a pale form in the corner of a cell— Muriel, on her own, her dress torn, blond hair bloodied. Devil's Bane curled around her body, streaming into her mouth. Thorns had scratched her skin, and red streaks marred her porcelain skin. Golden magic blazed around her body. Already, Kratos was using his magic to rip through the iron bars of the cell.

"Where is Adonis?" I demanded.

Hazel smacked my arm. "She can't talk, Ruby. Help her first, at least. You have plant powers, don't you?"

Right.

I rushed over to her, letting my fingers trace the Devil's Bane that trapped her. I didn't have much time to figure this out—I just had to get her out of here.

I closed my eyes, and energy buzzed from my stones. *Kill the angel,* the Old Gods sang....

I clenched my jaw. *Not now, fuckers.*

A feral snarl escaped my throat, and I flicked my fingers.

The vines began to retreat from her, snaking out of her mouth and away from her body. She fell to the floor, and Kratos swooped in to catch her.

A stream of drool trickled from the corner of her mouth.

Thunk. Thunk.

"Where is Adonis?" I shouted again.

"Underground," she rasped.

My stomach dropped. Underground? Gods below. What kind of torture had they subjected him to?

I bent lower, gripping her arm—maybe a little too tightly. "Underground where?"

She lifted a limp arm, pointing farther down the corridor. "There's a door in the ground." Her eyes fluttered closed again.

Kratos scooped her up, but I was already moving on, ahead of the others. Our bond pulled me toward him.

Thunk. Thunk.

After a few more yards, a metal hatch interrupted the stone ground. I yanked it up, revealing darkness and the dank smell of a grave.

Thunk — The sound of shattering glass stopped my heart. They'd broken through the shield.

With a racing pulse, I dropped into the hole—not entirely sure where I was going. As I dropped down, a terrible thought struck me. What if Muriel had been in on this? What if this was all part of their trap? After all—I was supposed to be their target.

When my feet hit the ground, a wave of fear slammed into me, silencing my thoughts.

Terrifying, spiked iron instruments lined the walls—a gallery of torture.

And there—in a shadowy corner—I found Adonis.

At the sight of him, the world tilted below my feet.

Nails pinned him to a wooden wall—nails driven through every inch of him, each one wrapped in Devil's Bane. The agony must have been unbearable.

My blood roared in my ears.

Blood streaked his golden skin, staining the floor. Only his perfect face was unmarred. His eyes were closed, dark lashes sweeping against his cheeks.

I heard nothing now except the beating of my own heart. A shock of guilt slammed into me, as if I'd been the one to do this to him. That vision I'd had of him—the one where I'd been tearing his flesh off his bones—I'd enjoyed it. I closed my eyes, trying to shut it all out.

"Ruby!" Yasmin's voice this time. "We have to get out of here."

"I know." Hot tears poured down my cheeks, but I forced myself to think logically. How would I get the nails out of him? I had control over plants, but definitely not iron.

I'd need some angelic intervention.

"Kratos!" I screamed.

He was by my side in the next moment, feet thudding on the stone floor. He still gripped Muriel in his arms.

"They're almost here—" He stopped short at the sight of Adonis.

"Can you get the nails out of him?" I asked, panic rising. "Fast?"

The angelic horde thundered over us, and Yasmin was yelling something about blocking the entrance.

Without another word, Kratos nodded, then launched into an Angelic spell. The words tumbled from his lips. They rattled chaotically in my mind, but I could see the spell working—drawing the nails from his body. They clattered to the floor, and Adonis's ruined body started to slump. I rushed forward, catching him in my arms.

Without the Devil's Bane, he could heal on his own. But with that poison coursing through his veins, he'd be out of commission for weeks, his body decaying....

Instinct took over, and I slid my arm under his neck. His blood soaked my clothes, and I pressed my mouth to his in a kiss. Gently, my lips moved over his, and my ancient magic ignited between us. As I kissed him, I could feel myself pulling the toxins from his body into my own. Devil's Bane wasn't poisonous to a fae—in fact, it filled me with a strange sort of energy.

I heard Adonis moan—a low sound, either pain or pleasure, and his tongue brushed against mine. His eyelids slowly opened, and his fingers moved over my arm, tightening. He pulled away from the kiss.

"Ruby," he whispered.

Hazel and Kratos were shouting, urging us to get going, but I had to make sure Adonis could move.

"Can you heal yourself now?" I asked.

Pain etched his features, and his dark magic began to writhe around his body. It skimmed over my skin—cold and soothing at the same time, like a blanket of night. Magic curled around us.

My gaze flicked to the ceiling, where Kratos had sealed the opening, buying us a little time.

"Are you okay?" I asked Adonis.

He pulled himself from my embrace, then rose to his full height. "Of course I am. I was doing fine."

"You've got to be kidding me."

"It's Muriel we need to worry about."

Kratos still held Muriel in his arms. "We can worry later. We need to leave now."

"Speaking of which," Hazel interjected. "How the fuck do we get out of here?"

Adonis pointed to the far side of the room, where an iron maiden stood before a bare stone wall. "I think there's a tunnel behind that wall that leads to the upper levels. I haven't had much chance to explore, but I spent three days listening to water drip behind the walls. I think I may have gone temporarily insane."

"Can someone smash through the walls?" asked Yasmin.

Adonis pulled Muriel from Kratos's arms to start healing her.

Kratos pressed his ear against the wall. Then, he backed away, chanting in Angelic.

As he did, the metal door above us groaned open, and panic tightened my throat.

They're here.

I closed my eyes, and warm light burst from my body. I vibrated with the magic of the Old Gods—with blood and moss and the forgotten secrets of buried bones. The beast, taking down the angels, light exploding from within me until I thought I might die from the power of it all.

This time, Hazel snapped me out of it with fingernails digging into my skin.

When I opened my eyes again, I stared at the shimmering shield above us, my body trembling. It had worked—at least, until Aereus broke through it again.

Thunk. Thunk.

"Let's move." Kratos stood before a crumbled wall—where rock and dust had crashed to the floor to reveal a hollow cavern.

As I ran for it, someone blocked my path. Adonis had healed Muriel completely. But unfortunately for me, she kind of looked like she wanted to murder me.

Her cheeks reddened, and she pointed at me. "You betrayed us."

"Not now, Muriel." I pivoted to move past her, but she grabbed me by the hair.

In the next moment, I found myself entangled in an avalanche of dress ripping, face-scratching, and hair-pulling.

Really? An angel who had witnessed Adam and Eve's fall in the Garden of Eden—and this was how she fought? Like a pissed off fifth-grader? Disappointing.

I shoved her hard, then punched her once in the jaw. She staggered back, her hand on her face. "You gave up our location to Aereus, didn't you, animal?"

"If she had," Adonis barked, "she wouldn't be here rescuing us, would she?"

Thunk. Thunk. Thunk.

Muriel went silent—pouting at me, pretty much—but she wasn't stopping me, at least.

I pushed past her, running with the others into a dark stone passage. Not just one passage—a network of dank tunnels that branched off around us like spokes on a wheel.

Around us, the palace's alarm bells rang loudly, reverberating in my skull. And once more, the sound of a shattering shield rang out.

The sound of Aereus's Angelic spells traveled to us, and as they echoed through the passage, a wall of flames rose up around us. Smoke billowed through the air, and I screamed for my sister.

Aereus wanted to burn us alive, and chaos reigned.

A powerful wave of Adonis's icy magic rippled through the passages, snuffing out some of the flames. Still, black smoke bloomed all around, and I doubled over, coughing uncontrollably.

"Hazel!" I choked out, tears streaming from my eyes.

Aereus's powerful voice boomed through the passage, and a fresh wave of flames roared around us, black smoke choking the oxygen out of the air.

A battle of Angelic words clattered and roared around me
—fire battling ice, the smoke only thickening.

"Hazel!"

A burst of coughing wracked my body, and smoke filled
my lungs, until dizziness clouded my mind completely.

🜲 10 🜲

I woke with a sharp intake of breath, filling my lungs with mercifully clear air. Iron dust covered my body, sapping my strength.

"Hazel," I gasped, but she wasn't near me. I was lying in Adonis's lap, looking up at his perfect face. He was still shirtless, and I could see the scars and gashes all over his chest. He'd hidden his midnight wings, making himself a little less conspicuous.

"Are you okay?" His gray eyes searched mine.

"Where's Hazel?" I rasped.

"Kratos got her out of the building. She's fine. You sucked in a lot of smoke."

The alarm bells still rang around us, and I pushed myself up to look around. We were in the marble hall with all the medieval art and confessional booths, and it seemed eerily still in here.

Adonis went still, frowning. "Someone's coming."

In the next moment, he was on his feet, pulling my hand toward one of the confessional booths. We hurried into it. It smelled of ancient wood in there, and light poured through the latticework onto ornate carvings in the dark oak.

A half-empty bottle of wine stood on a crooked chair. Seemed an angel had been indulging a bit in here.

In the cramped space, Adonis's powerful body pressed against mine. He leaned down, his dark power caressing me until I wanted to pull off my soot-covered dress and wrap my legs around him.

Focus, Ruby. You're about ten seconds away from death by angelic horde.

"I had a feeling you'd come for me here."

"I thought you were doing fine and didn't need me?"

He went quiet for a moment. "That's not entirely true."

"Once we get outside, I'll need you to fly out to the Jardin des Tuileries just long enough that we can make sure everyone is there. Then, we get out of France as fast as we can. But we need to wait until the coast is completely clear."

Outside, footfalls and the sounds of Angelic commands echoed off the ceiling. They were hunting for us, sending my heart into a wild race.

"I can hear your heart pounding," he whispered, warming my ear.

"Because my brain keeps trying to remind me of what Aereus will do to us if he finds us." I swallowed hard, and I traced my fingertips over one of the scars in his chest. Anger ignited when I thought of the agony Adonis must have endured. I wanted to drive nails right through Aereus until his enormous body ripped into pieces. Adrenaline surged through my veins. "Not to mention what he's already done to you."

Adonis stroked his hand down my chest, until it rested over my heart. "Calm yourself. You won't be able to think clearly if your emotions are overwhelming you."

Right. Panic was the enemy of strategy.

That said, the feel of Adonis's hand on my chest wasn't exactly calming—in fact, it sent my heart racing for a different reason. My breath sped up. "You're not helping me control my emotions, you know."

"I'm not?" he purred.

He traced his hand lower over my body, and warmth surged through my core. Heat and raw power radiated off his body. He was like a dark star, luring me in with his gravitational pull.

I shook my head. "Not exactly."

He stroked his fingertips down my spine, and my back arched.

"Well, Ruby. As much as I want to touch you in all the right places and listen to your heart race faster, maybe we should formulate a plan."

I was practically panting now. "Oh, yeah?"

"You're the one with the power of the Old Gods. And I know from personal experience that powerful emotions will cloud judgment and lead to ruin—"

"Wait, what? Just generally feeling emotions leads to ruination?"

"Just trust me."

"If there's a horseman equivalent of a psychologist, you might want to meet with one at some point."

He pulled away from me, and I regretted the loss of his warmth.

"Whatever you do," he said, "try to stay calm until we can get out of Paris. Don't think about Aereus's torture machines, or the nails he drove through my bones. Think about—whatever it is you think about when you get that faraway look in your eyes. I've watched you closely, and I've seen the smile on your lips while you think about *something*." His dark brows drew together. "What exactly is it that you think about?"

Nothing weird. You. Naked, with soup. "Plants."

"Plants."

I nodded.

"Funny," he said. "I think about the same thing."

"You do?" *Interesting, because mine was a lie.*

"When I need to master my emotions, I think about my garden. The anemones, the myrtle trees, the river. It's my home, the place that has belonged to me and always will."

"That's ... adorable. You daydream about your garden?"

"It requires my careful touch and my protection. It rewards me with beauty and comfort, and watching it thrive makes my heart joyful."

"You feel very strongly about your flowers. Careful, or gardening could lead to your ruination." I peered through one of the cracks, watching as the angels continued to stream through, searching for us.

"You'll need to glamour us to get us out of here." He looked through a crack. "Once the soldiers clear out of here."

"My magic won't work with all the iron dust covering my skin."

Adonis snatched the bottle of wine from the chair. "We'll just have to wash it off, then." He pulled down the top of my dress, exposing my bare skin beneath it. His exotic magic raised goosebumps on my skin, and even as the angelic soldiers hammered over the floor outside, I found myself completely transfixed by his eyes on my naked skin.

Adonis began pouring the wine over my chest and shoulders. Then he stroked his hand down my body, washing off the dust with the wine. Adonis tipped the bottle, and the red wine dripped over my body, washing off the dust with it.

As he did, I let my gaze roam over his body. I winced at the sight of his bare torso. His wounds were healing quickly, but I could still see every place where Aereus had gouged his skin with iron, all the divots and indentations. Aereus had scarred every inch of his golden skin.

"This must have been agony."

I expected him to brush it off like he usually did.

"It was," he said instead. He pulled my dress off the rest of the way, until I was standing in nothing but my underwear. Another slow pour of wine, and his hands roamed over my skin, washing off all the iron.

I reached up, brushing my thumb over his cheek. "When I kill Aereus, I'll make sure it's painful." In fact, I wanted to tear Aereus's head off his body and batter him to death with his own skull.

"At least my time here wasn't wasted."

"What do you mean?"

"Aereus has no idea how keen my hearing is," he said. "I listened in to his conversations with Johnny," he continued, letting the wine run over me. "And I know what they have planned. Aereus wants to call down an angel known as Metatron—ruler of the Heavenly Host."

With the iron washed off my bare skin, Adonis sat down on the bench. He pulled me onto his lap.

Slowly, he ran his fingertips inside the top of my panties.

"We need to get outside," I breathed.

"We will." He kissed my neck, and a hand ran up my thigh.

With his hands moving over my wet skin, I could hardly focus.

"Metatron," I repeated, trying to remember how to use words.

"The voice of the gods. Leader of the Heavenly Host. Ruthless."

His fingers moved higher, and my back arched. "Bad news, I take it?"

"He hates humanity," he added. "Hates demons, hates everything that can speak except angels."

Adonis's intoxicating scent curled around me, making my

skin hot, my knees weak. As I gazed at his perfect face, I found my tongue running over my lips, and Adonis seemed transfixed by the movement.

I felt his magic intensifying around me, thrumming up my spine and over my breasts.

Adonis leaned in closer, licking some of the wine off my neck. I wrapped my arms around his back.

"There," he said, his breath warming my skin. "All clean."

"Apart from the wine."

Another stroke of his tongue on my neck, and molten heat warmed me from the inside out.

"Adonis," I managed. "We need to go. They're waiting for us."

"We'll finish this later."

I rose and snatched my dress from the floor. I pulled it on. My underwear stuck to my wine-damp skin. It'd be a cold trip over the English Channel.

"Before we go out, I'm going to create another decoy. We can at least confuse the angels as much as possible."

I closed my eyes, letting my mind fill with images of the Garden of Eden and the scent of crushed grapes. The air felt heavy with rain. Then, I imagined Adonis—his golden skin, his tattoos, his pale gray eyes and graceful sweep of midnight wings.

I called to mind an army of him, each one physically perfect—except for the scarred skin. And by the side of each Adonis, I created a red-haired Ruby in her tattered dress.

I opened my eyes, then stood on my tiptoes to peer out the latticework window. There, outside, an army of us had stormed the Louvre. Aereus and Johnny would be completely confused. At least, I hoped.

"Want to have a look?" I asked.

Adonis peered outside and quirked a smile. "You can do this?"

"Not to brag, but I'm pretty amazing."

He frowned. "Is that how you see me?"

"Pretty good, right?"

"Not quite as devastating as the original, but you can work on it."

"This is why people get you confused with that dude who fell into the river looking at his own face."

"Narcissus. *Completely* different. Not nearly as good-looking."

"Stop talking. I need to glamour us now." I closed my eyes, and my body tingled as magic rippled over us.

I opened my eyes, and it was almost with a sense of regret that I watched him transform from a beautiful horseman into an ordinary angelic soldier. My own hair lightened from bright red to blond, my red-stained dress shimmering into a clean white gown.

When the glamour had completely taken hold, Adonis cracked open the confessional door, peering out. "Even with the illusions, we'll still have to move quickly. Johnny and Aereus will be able to smell you."

I stiffened. "Me in particular? Not you?"

"Fae have a particular smell. It wasn't so strong before, but with those gemstones, it's intensified."

This was news to me. "What do fae smell of, exactly?"

"Moss and dirt."

I blinked. "Is there not a better way you could have phrased that?"

"I happen to love the smell." He held up his hand, signaling for me to wait, until he whispered, "Now."

He pushed through the door into the hall, and we fell in line at a safe distance from the army of us. It was too bad I couldn't glamour them to smell like a forest floor, I supposed.

We broke into a run in the hall, moving among the illusions, until we reached an intersection of halls.

An angelic soldier burst from around the corner, slamming into me. I fell backward, and my head knocked against the hard marble floor.

The angel leapt on top of me, bloodlust glinting in his pale eyes. He sniffed the air, eyes shining.

✿ 11 ✿

I reached for the knife at my belt, but there was no need.

Above us, Adonis flicked his wrist. The motion severed the angel at the waist, and the remains of the angel's body slumped onto mine.

The angel's blood drenched my glamoured white dress, and my nostrils flared, stones heating in my forehead. My feral side *liked* the smell of angel blood a little too much, and I had to fight the disturbing urge to taste it. My canines lengthened, and I flicked my tongue over them.

Adonis pulled the angel's torso off of me, and I snarled, fighting to keep control of myself. "Do you have any tidier ways of slaughtering?"

"You're one to talk. I've seen how you kill." Blood had spattered him, too. "Anyway, he was trying to kill you, and I didn't have time to make it pretty."

I stood up and narrowed my eyes at him. His body was shaking, tense. Shadows darkened the air around him, and darkness clouded his eyes. I'd never seen him so rattled before. He'd always managed to convey a cool exterior.

Even through the glamour, I recognized something in him

that I knew well—but it was an emotion I'd never seen on Adonis before. Bloodlust. I'd been in that state enough times to know what he was thinking now. Something along the lines of *more death*.

"Adonis." I gripped him by the shoulders. "Focus."

The shadows cleared from his eyes, and his eyebrows drew together. He stared at the blood staining my body. For just a moment, he looked strangely vulnerable. Then his jaw clenched, as if he were gaining mastery of himself. "Right."

We started moving again, heading for the main entrance. Adonis slammed through the doors into the piazza. Around the pyramid, anarchy had erupted. Angelic soldiers were moving among the illusions of Adonis and me, trying to fight phantoms. Swarms of angels and cherubs darkened the skies above us, searching for the real Ruby and Adonis among all the fakes.

We moved among them unnoticed, racing now for our meeting spot in the Jardin des Tuileries, where Uthyr awaited us. My feet pounded hard against the stones, and my breath grew ragged.

Almost there. Almost free. Adrenaline sparked through my veins as I spotted the shimmering contours of the dragon, shielded by my glamour.

I'd done it. I'd gotten Adonis out of his prison, and we were escaping Aereus's clutches.

"There!" I shouted to Adonis.

Before we took off, I just needed to make sure we were all here, all accounted for.

I pulled the glamour off the dragon, my gaze roaming over Yasmin, Muriel, Kratos.... My heart hammered hard in my chest.

Where the fuck was Hazel?

"Hazel!" Kratos shouted.

I spun, following his gaze, and fear hit me like a freight train.

There—before the pyramid—the Horseman of Famine had captured my sister. Johnny's Angelic words boomed in the air around us, echoing off the stone. I stared in horror as his incantation created an iron mask for her mouth, a collar for her neck.

Johnny held an iron knife aloft, ready to plunge it into her heart. "A fae for a fae!" he boomed. He pressed the knife into her collar bone, drawing blood. Crimson streaked down the front of her body. "Give yourself up, Ruby," he screeched, "and your sister lives."

My mind flashed with the horror of what awaited me if I gave myself up to these two horsemen. But if not me, then it was Hazel. *Shit.* I was out of options here. But there was no way in hell I was letting Johnny take my little sister.

My body shook with a mixture of fear and rage, and I let my glamour drop. All at once, the army of Adonises and Rubys vanished. The wind toyed with my red hair, and I stood across from Johnny in my wine-stained, tattered dress.

Aereus and his angelic horde swarmed above, but as soon as my glamour dropped, angels began swooping lower, circling around me.

I thought I could hear Adonis saying something to me—shouting—but I tuned him out. I took a step forward, ready to announce myself.

Suddenly, the air around us erupted with angelic magic. I fell to my knees at the sound, clamping my hands over my ears. Adonis's voice rang out with Angelic spells, clashing with Johnny's. From behind me, Kratos joined in, and I felt as if my own mind were at war with itself.

The Angelic language in its true form, spoken by native speakers, was something humans and fae were never meant to hear. In the magical battle, angels' bodies began to drop from the skies, blood streaming from their ears.

Even with my hands clamped over my ears, the spells boomed through my fingers, driving me mad.

Angels were never meant to walk the earth.

The song of the Old Gods was swelling within me, reacting to the curse of the Angelic language. I needed to kill the angels, to slaughter all of them. The gemstones in my forehead began to heat, urging me on to massacre the angels around me.

I felt like a battle was raging between the Angelic language and the Old Gods, and I could hardly hear my own thoughts between them. All I knew right now was that I wanted blood—angel blood.

Stay in control, Ruby. Kratos used emotional pain to master his impulses. Maybe physical would work just as well.

I gritted my teeth, pulling the knife from my belt. I sliced through my palm, drawing blood. The sharp sting cleared the cacophony from my mind, and my senses sharpened. I stared at Johnny, seeing him clearly again. He'd dropped his grip on Hazel, but she still lay at his feet, bound in iron.

Now, blood poured from Johnny's eyes, his nose, his ears, as Kratos and Adonis attacked him with magic. He was screaming in Angelic, and by the look of it, trying to fight back with defensive spells.

With the iron clamped around her skinny body, she'd be in agony. Not to mention the knife wound at her collarbone.

The sight of her streaked with blood sent fiery wrath burning through my veins. I didn't just want to hurt Johnny now. I didn't just want to put him in the ground. I wanted him dead. The Old Gods wanted him dead, and they were going to help me.

My body ached to use the full force of their magic, to let

the light explode from my body. But I had to hold back. If I gave in to their desires completely, I'd die.

My gaze flicked to the skies, where Aereus circled among the other angels like a bird of prey. His Angelic words echoed off the stone walls.

Johnny was still on the ground, screaming out spells. I pulled the bow off my back and nocked an arrow, narrowing my eyes at him. I loosed two arrows in close succession, hitting him in his eye socket, then his throat. He fell to the ground, already succumbing to the effects of the Devil's Bane.

There's more where that came from, you skinny fuck.

I crossed to him, dropping the bow. I didn't need weapons now. In fact, I *was* a weapon—honed perfectly to destroy angels.

I licked my lips, already tasting blood. When I reached Johnny, he was grunting, struggling to stand. "I'm going to peel off your skin, fae whore!" he screeched.

I stepped over Hazel's prone body when I reached him, and I yanked him up by the throat. Strength infused my body, and I lifted him into the air, squeezing his neck until his remaining eye bulged.

"The Old Gods have a message," I said in a voice that wasn't quite my own. "You don't belong here. You never did. Humans, demons, fae ... we might be brutal and savage, but you created hell on earth."

He was screaming now, his shrieks music to my savage ears. I lifted my free hand to his face, and a dark smile curled my lips. Devil's Bane began to spool out of my fingernails, climbing into his mouth, his ears, his eye sockets. I sent the plants surging into his brain, suffocating it.

"You should have never come here with your Angelic language," I hissed. "None of you should have come."

I flicked my wrist, and Johnny's head exploded in a mist of flesh and bone.

One down, three to go.

I arched my back, feeling my canines lengthen. The Old Gods had awoken Feral Ruby, and she wanted more angel blood. I could end this all right here, get rid of them all.

I whirled, my gaze landing on the beautiful one with eyes the color of stormy skies. Already, Devil's Bane was spooling from my fingertips.

You're next.

I crossed to him, my body warming with light. I felt as if cracks were opening, ready to break me apart, ready to tear me to pieces.

You never should have come here.

But something in his eyes stopped me. I flicked my tongue over my teeth, transfixed by that flash of vulnerability in his eyes.

"Ruby."

As soon as he said my name, my mind began to clear again, the song of the Old Gods dimming to a hum.

Hazel. I needed to get her.

Just as I turned back to grab my sister, Aereus swooped down, his sword drawn.

My heart skipped a beat as he swung for Adonis.

Adonis raised his arm defensively, but it was too late. Blood arced through the air.

The Old Gods' gemstones sparked, urging me to use their power. Devil's Bane curled from my fingertips, reaching for Aereus. Even so, I knew it was too late.

Aereus had completely severed one of Adonis's arms, and he was lifting his sword again. Just as the tendrils of vines reached the Horseman of War, he brought his sword down again with a roar.

My mind went blank for a moment as horror slammed into me.

The horsemen couldn't kill each other, right? And yet—

the sight of Adonis, felled by Aereus's sword, robbed me of breath. His blood spilled over the stones.

I had a vague sense that Kratos was shouting something at me, but panic had begun to climb up my throat, and it was hard to think clearly.

Aereus turned to me, his angelic voice booming cursed spells. As he did, pain ripped my body apart, searing me from the inside out. Something was hitting me, again and again.

Clutching my ribs, I fell hard to my knees. I was dimly aware of blood spilling from my mouth, then of someone tugging me by the hair, lifting me from the ground like a trophy.

As my vision began to darken, only one thought rang in my mind, carving through the chaos of the angelic warfare. In fact, it rang out with a stark, crystal clarity. *Hazel and I are going to die here.*

❧ 12 ❧

Iopened my eyes a crack, and the light burned them. Stone arched above me. Pain splintered my body, so sharp I couldn't think through the haze of agony. Something felt very wrong inside of me, as if my insides had been punctured over and over. It took me a moment to realize they probably had been.

Was I alive or dead? Which was the better option?

The paradise of the Old Gods called to me—the untamed garden where no questions would plague my mind.

The air smelled of cedar.

Before I could focus on anything clearly, the world around me began to dim, replaced with a vision—my phantom life. The one with the cottage, and Adonis sitting naked before the fireplace. It seemed so vivid I could almost reach out and touch him....

THE NEXT TIME I OPENED MY EYES, THE PAIN HAD LEFT ME completely, replaced by a dull calm. Rosy sunlight streamed in through the windows—and with it, the wisteria from outside the castle climbed in through the opening. Once again, the plants had snaked over the floor, reaching for me.

I nearly missed the beautiful, dark-haired angel slumped in a chair in the shadows, his eyes closed. *Adonis.*

No wonder I felt better.

Drakon, his dragonile, sat on the floor next to him, thumping his reptilian tail against the floor. He blinked his yellow eyes at me, looking awfully proud at having contributed to his master's rescue.

Adonis's eyes opened, looking more haunted than ever. Something was very wrong.

My chest clenched. "Where's Hazel?"

"She's fine. She's here, at Hotemet." His voice sounded toneless.

I licked my dry lips. "What happened?"

"Aereus's sword carved me in half."

"I saw that."

"I got better, and I smelled your blood all around me. Aereus nearly killed you. He used his magic to destroy your body."

"So that's what that pain was." I swallowed hard. "How did I get out of there?"

"Kratos." He opened his mouth and closed it again, and his gaze shuttered. "It's over now."

There was something he wasn't telling me.

He leaned forward, resting his hands on his knees. "The important thing is that Metatron is on his way."

Is that what was bothering him? "Okay. I'll kill him, just like I killed Johnny. Vines. Exploding head."

Adonis shook his head. "He's not like Johnny. He's much more powerful, and he will toy with your mind."

I tried to sit up, but pain speared my ribs. Even with Adonis's healing magic suffusing my body, I still felt like I'd been sliced open through my middle. Like my organs had been taken out, beaten up a bit, and stuffed back in.

A cough wracked my chest, and for a split second, I had the disturbing feeling that my intestines were about to fall out of place. I grimaced, clutching my gut. *Gods save me.*

Adonis rushed for the edge of my bed, his magic thickening in the air. "Lay down." A sharp command.

"I don't understand," I managed. "Last time I got hurt, I healed fast. And your magic has always healed me instantly in the past. Why is it not working now?"

"Aereus used powerful spells on you. It's a miracle you're alive at all." He frowned, tracing his fingertips over the stones in my forehead. "If it weren't for these, I think you'd be vaporized right now."

I winced at the image. "Let's not dwell on that image too long, shall we?"

Adonis whispered under his breath in Angelic. His healing magic skimmed over my skin, taking the pain away and making my eyelids droop. As the agony left my body, a hint of euphoria washed over me. I could already smell the garden of Paradise. I reached for Adonis, but he pulled away from me.

"There's something you're not telling me," I managed.

That cold, haunted look in his eyes shut me up. "Get some sleep."

A command I couldn't refuse. When I closed my eyes, I was in the garden again.

❧

As I slept, I was dully aware of Hazel's voice telling me long, rambling stories of her time in the dragon's lair.

I woke fully again at night, with moonlight streaming into the room onto Adonis. It silvered his skin and sparked in his pale eyes. "Ruby," he said quietly.

"How long has it been since we returned from Sadeckrav?" I asked.

"Three days. How are you feeling?"

Slowly, I pushed myself up onto my elbows. Now, only a dull pain throbbed in my ribs. "Fine. But let's cut to the chase. What's going on with Metatron? I need more details."

"I spotted him at the Tower of London with one or two members of the Heavenly Host. When I haven't been here, watching over you, Kratos and I have been spying on him. We've seen him moving around the city, trying to meet secretly with other angels."

My throat tightened. "The Tower of London? That's where the Institute is located."

"Not anymore."

My breath sped up. "What about Yasmin's daughter?"

He nodded. "As soon as we returned here, she was reunited with the surviving members of the Institute. I helped her find her daughter, who was hiding out in the rookeries with her uncle."

"She's okay? Thank the gods."

"Yasmin was out of her mind when she heard what had happened. Metatron wanted to make a point about revolutions and submission to authority. The Tower walls are now decorated with the severed heads of members of the Institute. Only because of luck did Yasmin's daughter make it out of there alive."

I rubbed my eyes. "Okay, so you know where the Heavenly Host are hidden now? If we find them, you can just kill them all. Then we're done."

"I'm afraid it's not that simple."

Something in his tone sent a lick of dread up my spine. "What do you mean?"

"Metatron isn't an ordinary angel. He's the one who cursed Azazeyl when he fell. He's the one who split the fallen angel into seven earthly gods, damned to their own hells. He's the one who tasks the horsemen with destroying humanity. Frankly, he's a bit unpleasant."

"So what's he doing?"

"He's making his soldiers immortal. One by one. I can't kill them."

Panic began climbing up my throat. With an army of immortals, we didn't stand a chance. I needed to try my light magic again. "Let's go to the Tower."

"Can you even sit up?"

A sharp pain hit my side. Okay, so I couldn't just sit upright like that, using my abdominal muscles. Grunting, I rolled to the left. From there, I could push myself up with my arm until I was nearly sitting, as long as I didn't shift too much to the side—

"Balls!"

"You're not ready for this."

Almost up. "We need to end this now. If Metatron wins, I'll be dead. So I think a bit of abdominal discomfort is manageable."

Adonis quirked an eyebrow. "Have you mastered your light magic?"

Not even close. Still pretty sure the Old Gods wanted to kill me. "No, but I have to try before this immortal army gets any bigger." Wincing at the pain in my gut, I pushed myself off the bed to a standing position using my arms. And I nearly toppled over. "By the time we reach London, I'll be feeling much better. Just hit me with some of your opiate magic on the way." I gripped my stomach. "Any chance you can just defeat his immortality spell with a mortality spell?"

Adonis shook his head. "Metatron's Angelic spells are too powerful. He's the voice of the gods." Then, he fixed his gaze on me. "The magic of the Old Gods is the only thing that can combat him." A muscle tightened in his jaw. "If we let him continue, we won't stand a chance. There will be no way to defeat his army."

"There's a small chance I might start to lose my mind when I use the Old Gods' magic." And also ... I might die. "If I start to look like I'm losing control, I need you to hurt me."

He scowled. "I'll handle you without hurting you. But you'll need to be fast. Blast him with that magic before he gets the chance to smell you. Just like you did when you blasted the Heavenly Host off the earth last time. If it starts to go wrong, and if the Old Gods start taking over, I'll stop you."

"Of course. Yes. I smell like the underside of a rock, so I need to be fast."

"Remember, magic doesn't have its own will. Someone always commands it. When I died, it was because the Old Gods wanted me dead. They were in control. You need to control their power instead. You need to command it, to direct it."

"How?"

"Make it a part of you."

Right. I had no idea how to do that, but considering the fate of the entire world was at stake, I had to at least try.

✤ 13 ✤

lamoured as ravens, we swooped over the ruined city of London, the wind whipping at our skin. Steel-gray clouds covered the sky.

At the sight of the ravaged husks of buildings below us, a chill rippled over my skin. Things had gotten worse since I'd last been here. Yasmin had said that people were starting to organize, to get ready to fight back against the angels. Behind these crumbling walls, were people really willing to fight?

I tightened my arms around Adonis's back, my gaze sweeping over his features. He'd hardly spoken at all on our way here. Something had happened in Paris that he wasn't telling me, and it was starting to drive me crazy.

"Have you ever met him?" I asked.

"Who?"

"Metatron."

"Once. It was enough."

As we soared closer to the Tower, I caught a glimpse of a legion of angelic soldiers marching along Bethnal Green Road. Their weapons and armor gleamed in the dull light. It was a neighborhood I knew well—one of squat buildings, old pubs mixed with trendy new bars—all deserted since the Great Nightmare had begun. But as the angelic horde marched, I watched the structures crumble around them. Buildings shook, windows shattered, and pieces of plaster rained into the road.

Immortals.

The pavement cracked beneath the marching army.

My breath sped up. "What's happening to the buildings?"

Adonis's grip tightened on me, and he pulled me so close I could feel his heart beating through his clothes. "The Angelic language is used to create reality. It seems that Metatron is using it to break reality apart. He's practicing creating chaos."

I swallowed hard. "He wants to destroy it all, is that it? Everything on earth."

"Not exactly." A muscle clenched in his jaw. "First, he plans to make us suffer."

I shook my head. "Why?"

"Because we haven't sufficiently worshipped him, and it irritates him."

"So he's just an ordinary insecure asshole. Except he's also a godlike being with the power to destroy the fabric of the universe."

"That sums it up."

We flew further south, toward the Tower, and the swarm of angels kept marching through the street as steel bent and cement cracked around them.

At last we reached the Tower, and nervousness crawled up my spine. What kind of monster were we dealing with here?

"I can feel his power." A dark whisper from Adonis.

Was it just me, or was the Horseman of Death himself freaking out right now? That did nothing to assuage my nerves. Considering we didn't have a ton of hope, I wasn't going to tell him my own disturbing secret—the one about how the Old Gods wanted me dead.

"If we get close to him," said Adonis, "you'll need to act quickly. Even when you're glamoured, he'll be able to smell you."

"Right. Moss and dirt. Thanks for reminding me of that."

We swooped over the Tower walls, Adonis's wings beating like a heart.

"There," he said. "He's in the Tower church."

We dove lower over the Tower green—over the spot where traitors, heretics, and unwanted wives had fed the stones with their blood.

Angels milled around us, their bodies glowing with golden light.

We touched down on the cobblestones just in front of the church entrance. The iron gate and doors stood open, and pale light streamed out of the archway.

Already, I could feel Metatron's power thrumming over my skin. It felt alien—an invasive magic that belonged in the celestial realm. Not here.

As we stood at the precipice, my heart rate began to speed up, pulse racing. I had to remind myself that Metatron would see only a simple raven if he looked our way. One of many in the Tower. Not a big deal.

We took a step inside, and my breath caught at the sight before me. There, at the altar, stood Metatron. Golden wings cascaded from his back, which was turned toward us, and an angel knelt before him. The angel spoke in Angelic, so I had no idea what he was saying, but he seemed to be supplicating himself. He clasped his hands together, his head lowered before Metatron, like he was worshipping him.

Seemed like Metatron had found someone willing to pander to his overwhelming insecurity.

As we stood in the church's doorway, Metatron held out his hands to either side, and pearly, celestial light glowed from his body. He arched his back, and his powerful voice began to boom around us, echoing off the church's stone walls. He spoke in Angelic, and the raw power of the words pounded through my bones. As he chanted his spells, thin rays of light beamed from his skull. And everything the light touched began to disintegrate and dissolve, bits of the walls and ceiling crumbling to the floor.

My breath caught in my throat. I needed to see his face.

The angel at his feet seemed enraptured, his lips curled in an ecstatic smile. From the church walls, pieces of stone began to break, and cracks opened in the flagstones. As I listened to the spell, chaos rampaged through my skull— words and fragments of words, all disconnected, all jumbled and meaningless. *Pyramid puddle can open half luck mugger stem alter mag ord lish lake minst....*

I clamped my hands over my ears, trying to block out the chaos.

When Metatron had finished his spell, Adonis tugged on my arm, signaling that I had to hurry up. But I felt rooted in place, desperate to see his face.

I got my wish then. Metatron turned around, and the breath left my lungs.

Apart from the color of his wings, he looked nearly *exactly* like Adonis. Same gray eyes, same breathtaking beauty. But there was something colder about Metatron, something more alien. It was a divine beauty that simple, bestial creatures like me were never meant to see. *Never meant to be here.*

I took a steadying breath and stepped farther into the church. To Metatron, I still appeared as a raven, but I knew I only had a matter of seconds before he smelled me.

Now, the stones in my forehead began to tingle. The scent of a lush garden curled around me. Metatron's Angelic words clattered in my mind, but as the light began to warm up my body, it drowned out some of the chaos of his spells.

I stared at him—at this creature who didn't belong here—

and rage begin to roil in my chest. The Old Gods didn't want him here, and a chorus of their voices rang in my mind. The Old Gods wanted to teach him a lesson, wanted to teach all the angels a lesson. It was something we should have done long ago, when they came to the Garden of Eden, when they brought their invasive magic to our world. Should have hunted them, fertilized the Garden with angel blood.

My canines began to lengthen. *Kill all of them.* My back arched, and light began to burst from my body, cracking through my skin. Here, I'd explode like a dying star.

I snarled, light beaming from my body, prepared to slaughter—

All at once, a soothing magic slipped into my mind, calming my rage. It was a blanket of night, of sleep, of the quietness of soil....

The chorus of the Old Gods dulled in my skull, and it took me a moment to realize that a beautiful man had wrapped his arms around me, and that he smelled like myrrh.

I blinked, realizing I was in the air. Adonis's arms were tight around me, and the fresh air outside kissed my skin.

I swallowed hard. "So, I guess that didn't go well. What happened, exactly? Did you see—did I look different?" Had he noticed that light was ripping me apart from the inside out, and that the Old Gods were trying to kill me?

"You were starting to attack me. I had to intervene."

Shit. "But my body looked normal."

He frowned. "I tell you that you were trying to kill me, and you're concerned about how your body looked?"

"I was just curious if the magic made me look different."

"Apart from the terrifying rage in your expression, no. Why?"

"I don't suppose I killed Metatron while I was at it?"

"No, but he shot a moderately annoyed look at you, like he didn't want a raven in his church."

"That's it? The Old Gods were screaming in my mind about angel blood fertilizing the Garden of Eden, and all I achieved was moderate annoyance?"

Adonis cocked his head. "He is very powerful. You'll need more time. Or more mastery. Or more ... something. We'll work on it."

Adonis's skin looked paler than it should. No longer golden, it had taken on a porcelain hue, as if some of the blood had been drained from his body.

I touched his cheek. "Are you okay?"

"I'm fine. It's just that I think your magic affected me a little more than it did Metatron. I'll recover."

In the chilly air over the Tower of London, I scanned Adonis's perfect features, cold gray eyes, and dark eyelashes. "He's connected to you, isn't he? He looks just like you."

For a moment, a heavy silence fell over us. Then, without meeting my gaze, Adonis said, "He created me."

"But you had a mother." I blinked. "Do you mean he's your father?"

"I suppose you could call it that."

✦ 14 ✦

Ever since our battle at the Louvre, I'd had the sense that Adonis had been keeping something from me. He was no longer flirtatious or seductive, no longer making eye contact. For some reason, he'd become colder and a little more distant, like something was haunting him.

When we returned from the Tower, he walked me to my room with shadows darkening the air around him, giving one-word answers to my questions.

Was it some kind of angelic daddy issues that had him acting strangely? I had no idea. But after a few hours of stewing in my room, I decided I should just ask him. We were supposed to be working together, weren't we? I needed to know the truth from him.

I crossed through the drafty stone hall toward his room, where I found the door slightly ajar. It creaked as I pushed it open further. I didn't see any signs of Adonis in here—just Drakon, sitting in the corner, lazily thumping his scaly tail up and down on the stone. He lifted his head, blinked his yellow eyes at me a few times, then fell back asleep.

Still, I could feel Adonis's power crackling over my body.

It was only when I heard the running of water that I understood he was filling the tub.

"Adonis?" I called out.

"I'm in here." His voice came from an archway.

I felt torn between an overwhelming urge to see what he looked like in the bath, and my better judgment that told me maybe this was weird. I'd never actually slept with him. Maybe we weren't in "chatting in the bath" territory yet. "I'll come back later."

"It's fine."

Or maybe we were.

I crossed through the doorway, and found Adonis shoulder-deep in an enormous, circular stone tub. Light spilled in from latticed windows onto him, giving him a sort of halo.

He gripped a bar of soap, and given the redness of his skin, it looked like he'd been scrubbing at it. His dark tattoos snaked over his raw skin.

"What's wrong?" I asked.

"We just have a lot ahead of us if we're going to combat the chaos Metatron is creating." Steam curled the air around him.

My eyes swept over his muscled torso. "I'm not a psychologist, but I'm getting the sense that your father's presence here is bothering you."

"I have a mother. I don't have a father. Metatron impregnated my mother, just like he impregnated the mothers of Kratos, Johnny, and Aereus, but...."

"They're your half-brothers?"

A slow shrug. "If you want to call it that."

I crossed to him, sitting at the edge of his bathtub. I let my fingertip trail in the steaming water. It was practically scalding.

Droplets of water dotted his skin, and I had the strongest urge to lick them off.

Slowly, he raised his gaze to meet mine, and the raw vulnerability in his gray eyes pierced me to the core.

I cocked my head. "That's the first time you've looked at me since we returned from the Louvre. I mean really looked at me."

"Angels are cruel, cold creatures from the vast, unchanging landscape of the heavens. I've seen civilizations rise and fall, cities born only to crumble. I've seen the birth and death of gods. I speak a language humans were never meant to learn, and I kill people just by feeling too much." There was no feeling in his words now, no emotion. Just a cold, stark reality. "It's in my nature to kill and to destroy. It's what I was born to do."

"Bullshit. We're not born to do anything. We make ourselves. I'm a fae, a succubus, a spy, a demon. I'm a god and a beast, a dancer and a soldier. I wasn't born to be any one thing, and neither were you. We are what we create. We are our actions and our stories."

A slow tilt of his head, his eyes now pure ice. "And killing is what I do."

"Why is this coming up now? What happened?"

"When you flew over Paris, did you see the humans camped out in the fields? They lived in makeshift tents and huddled around bonfires. Mothers, fathers, children, babies...."

"Yeah. I remember. I saw some little kids toddling among the gardens."

"They're all dead now. You need to understand. Nature is cruel, and so am I."

My chest clenched. "How? Why?"

"I told you that powerful emotions can lead to ruination. If I feel too much, people die. When I found my mother's dead body, waves of death rippled off me. I slaughtered the entire city of Afeka nearby. I walked through the streets and found the dead littering the cobblestones. Young and old. And when I recovered at the Louvre, I smelled your blood all around me. I could no longer hear you through our bond. I was certain they'd killed you. You're still mortal. I couldn't control it, and a wave of death washed over the city. Our souls are immutable, Ruby. You might appear to be a succubus, a dancer, a soldier, but I've seen the real you."

I wanted to tear my gaze away from the pain in his eyes. "Enlighten me."

"The real you is wild and beautiful. And while you take on all these disguises, you're running from yourself. I can see it in your eyes sometimes. Fantasies draw you in. You're imagining a paradise that never existed, a Ruby that never existed."

I clenched my jaw, thinking of the fae I'd seen in the cottage. The happy couple, making soup. "Paradise does exist, it's just not handed to us on a plate. It's something we create. Did you see those two fae living in the cottage, when we were on our way to meet Kratos? It might not be a palace or a tropical island or whatever, but their simple life right now seems like paradise to me. That could be us."

"Us? When it's my destiny to slaughter thousands just by feeling emotions?"

I crossed my arms. "This 'my destiny is to slaughter' thing is horseshit. If it was your inescapable destiny, you'd be doing it constantly. When was the last time you lost control and killed people?"

"A thousand years, maybe." He seemed lost in his own mind. "But it's just that rage poured off me when I thought you were dead. I think a part of me wanted everyone to die. The bloodlust was uncontrollable." He straightened, the water dripping off his skin in rivulets. "Has it occurred to you that maybe you're lying to yourself about what you really are? Do you really think you can just reinvent yourself, that you can just wipe the slate clean and start again? I've seen you covered in the blood of angels. I've seen you rip into flesh. That's the real you, and it terrifies you."

Irritation simmered. "You don't get to define me."

He traced his fingertip through the water, creating little ripples. "You're right. Just make sure you're not running from the darkest parts of you. You have a tendency to romanticize things."

He was annoying me now. "What makes you say that?"

"The fae you saw in the woods, the ones you think live in Paradise. I could smell the blood on them. Human and fae blood. They'd been eating their own species. How do you think they survived in this world? By being brutal and savage, the way nature designed them."

My stomach dropped. *No way.* "Blood could have been there for any reason."

"I should just let you believe in your fantasies, shouldn't I? It's almost heartbreaking to disabuse you of them. You have such a vibrant phantom life."

I swallowed hard. His words weren't *entirely* off the mark —in fact, he knew what I called my other life. And it did sometimes seem that my phantom life—the one with the garden and the cottage—was more real than the grim world around me.

"There's nothing wrong with having an active fantasy life."

He cocked his head, studying me intently. "What is that you see in your fantasies, anyway?"

The whole "soup fantasy" was a little embarrassing, and yet I felt an overwhelming urge to confess it. Like I just needed to get it off my chest. "You, eating soup by a fireplace." My cheeks heated. "Naked."

Not weird at all.

A wicked smile. "And that's the first problem with an

active fantasy life. It pulls you away from the truth. I don't even like soup."

Of course the Horseman of Death did not sit by fireplaces with hot soup.

I hadn't convinced him of anything, but it seemed like maybe he'd lost the will to argue with me. I didn't want to argue with him anymore, either. Right now, I felt sick of talking, sick of words. I just wanted the peacefulness of an empty mind.

He leaned back, his stormy gaze boring into me. "Tell me more about this naked fantasy you have of me."

At those words, all I knew was that I really wanted was to feel his body beneath mine.

"It's more about the soup, honestly," I lied. "Minestrone." I licked my lips.

"I don't even know what that is. Do we have to focus on the soup aspects of this fantasy?"

Slowly, I tugged up the hem of my dress, showing off my thighs. "But it has parmesan and pancetta."

"I don't care about the pancetta. Keep pulling up your dress."

I lifted it another inch. "And zucchini. *Diced.*"

He gripped the edge of the tub. "Dress. Off."

"Some recipes call for butter." I pulled off my dress entirely, and the cool air whispered over my skin.

Adonis's body seemed to stiffen, his gray eyes brightening. "That's more like it."

"Your bath looks nice." The feel of his eyes on my body was electrifying.

I unhooked my bra, letting it fall to the floor. My body warmed, and I felt as if my breasts were swelling under his gaze.

Adonis's jaw dropped open, and he drank me in. My thighs clenched with anticipation. Then, I slid off my panties.

I stepped into the bath, the water scalding my porcelain skin until it turned pink. My legs slid against his as I lowered myself into the tub.

I nestled in across from him. His magic thrummed hot over my skin, and despite the warmth around me, goose-bumps rose on my skin. "I said we can create Paradise, right? I'll show you."

I summoned glamour, transforming the air around us to create an illusion of blood red flowers—the same ones that lined the riverbed in Afeka. Then, I flicked my fingers, and the sparkling river appeared, curving out of the cavern of the afterworld. Adonis's home—and the home of the Old Gods. With a twitch of my fingers, myrtle trees sprang up around the river's edge.

For just a moment, I thought I glimpsed drops of blood on their leaves, but I blinked, shoving the image out of my mind. Something dark nagged at the recesses of my mind, but I ignored it, letting my leg slide against Adonis's.

A little more life glinted in his eyes now—a little hunger—and his mouth twitched in a dangerous smile. Sensuous magic pulsed off him, swirling around my body along with the steam. Deep within the eyes of an immortal being like him, you could find a union of opposites: hot and cold, dark and light, the beginning and the end.

My core throbbed at the sight of him. I'd never wanted someone so badly in my life.

"What other sort of paradise can you create for me?" His voice had become husky. His heavy-lidded eyes promised sex and danger all at once.

I flicked my wrist, and the vision of the garden disappeared, replaced by a steaming bowl of soup.

A short growl. "Not food."

The soup's surface glimmered red, and I frowned. I

snapped my fingers, and the disturbingly crimson soup disappeared.

Adonis gripped the soap in his hands and leaned forward. With a gentle touch, he started soaping my skin, sliding his hands up my calves.

His fingertips lightly stroked my legs as he washed me, and I felt my knees falling open, inviting him in.

My breath came in short, sharp bursts, and I couldn't really focus on the illusions anymore. Not with the hungry look he was giving me. My body began to tremble with anticipation, legs opening wider. His hands moved farther up my thighs. I ached for him to keep going.

I wanted more contact with him, wanted to feel him inside me. But he was holding back. His powerful body skimmed against mine, his touch light. Already, I was arching into him, aching for more. His soapy thumbs brushed over my hardened nipples, a light touch that made my back curve into him. *More, more, more....* I moaned lightly.

Painfully slowly, he lowered his mouth to my throat, his lips hot against my skin. He was tasting me, exploring.

A louder moan this time. He lifted his face for a moment, gazing at me from under his dark lashes, a smile curling his lips. He was enjoying teasing me.

I wrapped my arms around his neck, my legs around his. He growled softly, skimming his hands farther up my body to cup my breasts. Liquid heat pulsed in my core, and I pulled him in closer to me. I rocked against him, feeling the hardness of his body.

His powerful back tensed, and then he whispered in my ear, "Not so fast. I'm going to take my time with you."

I didn't want him to take his time. I wanted him now, hard and fast. I stroked my hands down his back, feeling his body go rigid under my fingers. Then, I found his mouth with mine, pulling him in for a deep kiss. My tongue brushed against his, my hips moving against him, more urgently.

I smelled the scent of an exotic garden curling around me. *Paradise is here.*

My kiss deepened, desperate now. I *needed* him. "Adonis," I whispered.

I raked my fingernails down his back, then gripped his ass. I pulled him closer, guiding him into me. When he'd buried himself inside me, filling me completely, I moaned loudly, spurred on by pure need. My body tightened around him.

He stroked slowly between my legs, and I had the vague sense that I was moaning his name over and over. As ecstasy claimed my body, I could no longer quite remember how language worked.

As I shuddered against him, only one word rang in my mind. *Paradise.*

❦ 15 ❦

We sat at the round dining table in the Celestial Room, with moonlight washing over us. There were four of us, joined together to discuss our plan of attack: Kratos, Yasmin, Adonis, and I.

I swirled the wine in my glass, thinking about the terrifying chaos Metatron could create using only his words. Now that we knew Metatron could create immortal angels, we had to come up with something. Fast.

Kratos glowed with golden light, gripping his wineglass so tightly it looked like it might break. "I am Conquest. I was born to lead an army. I can command legions of soldiers to victory at my behest and force my enemies into submission. I can orchestrate a large-scale attack using my mind, and subjugate our enemies. Only problem is that I'm several legions short of an army." He met my gaze. "What about your powers? Those gemstones? You managed to get the Heavenly Host off the earth once. Why can't you do it again?"

Because I'd die.

I shook my head. "I don't have control over that magic yet. It's too powerful for me. I'm working on it, but I need more time. If we can just do something to buy us time, then I'll be able to fight them." I paused, tapping my fingertips on the table. "This situation is admittedly not awesome. And neither of you happen to know any Angelic spells that could combat Metatron's magic? Can you make his army mortal, at least? Then Adonis could kill them."

"No," said Adonis. "Metatron is the voice of the gods. His Angelic is pure and perfect, and our magic won't combat him. Only you could do that, I think, with your light magic."

"The magic I can't control whatsoever?" I frowned. "Okay. How about we create an army? What about all the humans just barely clinging onto life in the rookeries and hovels around the country? They'll fight to survive." Granted, they might not want to follow the angel who'd been hunting them, but maybe we could persuade them somehow.

Yasmin shook her head. "Humans won't save us. We break a little too easily. We need to make our army out of demons."

"We don't exactly have a great relationship with the demon world," said Adonis. "And moreover, we can't kill the Heavenly Host anyway. They're immortal, remember?"

My throat tightened. "No, but we could buy ourselves some time. We can slam them all with Devil's Bane arrows and bullets and knock them out for weeks. Maybe during that time, I can learn to control my powers better."

"Frankly, that's the best we can hope for right now." Yasmin leaned on the table. "And what if I told you we could make our human allies a little more durable? That we could find someone to transform them into demons and fae?"

I cocked my head. "How is that possible?"

Yasmin paced over the flagstones, her brow furrowed. After Metatron's attack on the Tower, she seemed more determined than ever to help put an end to the Great Night-mare. "Azazeyl's power can do it."

I'd seen the statue of Azazeyl at Adonis's castle—the

beautiful, pensive man with a snake coiled around his thigh. Maybe I'd seen him once or twice in my fantasies, too. He'd been the one to tempt Eve in the Garden of Eden. He was the one who brought the Angelic language to earth in the first place.

And yet ... had she lost her mind? He didn't exist anymore. "He fractured into seven gods when he fell to earth. There is no Azazeyl."

She cocked her head. "Before he fell to earth, he visited the Garden of Eden, and he fathered a child with a human. His descendant lives, and she has the power to transform humans into demons."

"Who is this person?" Kratos asked.

"Our sources tell us that her name is Rosalind, and she lives in the Vampire Kingdom of Lilinor with a demigod named Caine. Grandson of Nyxobas. At least, they used to be vampires."

"Caine," said Adonis. "He's awful."

"What are you talking about?" I asked. "I've heard of him. My boyfriend, Marcus, was once a soldier in Caine's army. Caine is apparently mind-blowingly hot, and—" I stopped short, reading Adonis's irritated expression. "That's not important. He's a general and whatnot."

Adonis glared at me. "He's the demon who seduced Muriel five centuries ago. He intended to ruin her. He hates angels. And of course he does, because he's an incubus."

Yasmin let out a long sigh. "Well, his wife has the power of seven gods. So whoever Caine shagged four centuries ago will just have to deal with it."

Kratos rubbed his forehead. "Will the humans even agree to this? To become demons? And would the humans even agree to work with us after...."

He let the words die on his tongue—the likely words being something like *I hunted them like rats through the streets.*

Adonis looked at me. "You spent time in the rookeries. You know humans just like Yasmin does. What do you think?"

I drummed my fingertips on the table. "Kratos has a bit of a problematic reputation among the human populations, since his dogs had a habit of eating them."

Kratos's features darkened. "I hope they appreciate the sacrifice I've been making. My hounds have been starving on a diet of pigs."

I nodded. "I'm sure the humans will be very impressed."

"So you don't think it will work?" asked Adonis. "Our transformed army?"

I bit my lip. "I think they'll come around, eventually. We'll need to keep Kratos out of it until the humans are already committed. But when it comes down to it, I think they'll fight for their own survival."

"I think you're right," said Yasmin. "The will to live is a powerful thing."

"So where is this vampire kingdom?" asked Adonis.

Yasmin leaned on the table. "It can only be accessed through a portal. It's one of the magical realms, completely sealed off from this world ever since they battled the magic-hunters years ago. Someone will need to find a way in."

"I'll do that," said Kratos. "It will give you all some time to convince the humans to let me lead them while I'm not here, terrifying them with my presence. But are you sure Rosalind has this ability?"

Yasmin nodded. "One of our informants was a member of Caine's army when Rosalind transformed them all. He was once a vampire. Now, he's a hellhound." She chewed on her thumbnail. "Now, I just need to meet with some of the human leaders and convince them we're on their side." She shot me a piercing look. "I looked for your old friends, just like you asked, to see if we could better make inroads into the resistance. Your friend Alex ranks highly among them. He returned from his safe haven outside of London. Do you think he trusts you?"

I loosed a relieved breath. *He's safe.* "I'm not sure." Guilt pierced my chest. "He did at one point. We were close, even. But I disappeared when I started working for the Institute. He had no idea what I was doing. The last time I saw him, I was on a parapet with Johnny, aiming an arrow at him. Adonis helped to spare his life, so maybe he'd be willing to talk to us."

"We'll explain to him that you were working for us." She tapped her fingertip against her lip. "I'll try to arrange a meeting with the resistance leaders and Alex. You go on your own. No horsemen. It will be easier to persuade them without any apocalyptic agents milling around. And without me, for that matter."

16

High above the streets, I clutched tightly to Adonis's neck. Under a starlit sky, we soared over London's perimeter, over the crumbling, shattered buildings, the abandoned streets. Empty cars littered the roads, gleaming in the moonlight. At night, I didn't even need to glamour us. Adonis's magic had us blending into the night sky like dark smoke.

Already, we were soaring over London's western edge. As we flew above an enormous Victorian cemetery, my pulse raced. Even from here I could see many of the graves had been disturbed, and piles of dirt lay next to dark holes.

My lip curled with disgust. Humans sometimes resorted to cannibalism in times of desperation, but they couldn't be surviving off old corpses. Right? I suppressed a shudder, burying the thought deep under the surface.

Then, I hugged Adonis a little closer. "It's nice of you to give me a ride, but I could have gone with Yasmin."

Adonis's powerful arms tightened around me, and he lowered his face to mine. "I want to stay as close to you as possible."

"I do have the power of the Old Gods protecting me."

"It didn't help you in Paris, did it?"

An image flashed in my mind—Adonis, falling beneath Aereus's sword, his body carved in two. "I was a little distracted. I saw the Horseman of War cut your head in half."

"Is that what threw you off? You were worried about me?"

"Yes."

"That's absolutely ridiculous. I can't die. Unless you kill me."

The very thought of it made my stomach flutter. "I know. But it looked like you died, and it was very visceral. It was an emotional reaction."

His midnight wings beat the air. "Has it occurred to you that we might be bad for each other?"

Cold wind rippled over me. "What do you mean?"

"You worry about me so much that you no longer can protect yourself, and I worry about you so much that I slaughter everyone around me. Not to mention the fact that you are the one living being who can kill me. We make each other vulnerable."

"That's what love is, my friend." As soon as the words were out of my mouth, my cheeks heated.

He pulled me in closer. "Is that right?" He honestly looked almost perplexed, as if this were some kind of foreign concept. "Yes, I think you're right."

"You're old as hell. You've never been in love before?"

"I thought it was a human concept. I didn't think it was something a horseman could feel." Warmth radiated from his powerful body. "But now you feel like my home, and like you've always belonged to me." His voice was a velvet caress that tingled over my skin.

My lips curled in a smile. "So how do I rank against your garden?"

"I'd say you have the advantage."

I nestled my head into his neck. I probably didn't need him flying with me to London. I could disguise myself completely. But the truth was that I liked his protectiveness. I liked that he wanted to keep me safe—just like I wanted to keep him safe. It had been a long time since anyone had tried to look after me.

As if hearing my thoughts, Adonis said, "Use our bond to stay in touch with me. I'll stay out of the way while you're meeting with the humans, but I won't go far."

"I will."

Westminster was our designated meeting point. While Metatron had taken over the Tower in the East, some of the humans had retreated to the old Anglo-Saxon part of the city. They'd taken over the Houses of Parliament and Westminster Cathedral, planning their resistance from there.

And as soon as we touched down in Westminster, Adonis was supposed to take off. When trying to persuade humans that we were on their side, we didn't need Death hanging around, glooming up the place.

As we swooped lower over Westminster, I found the old medieval buildings almost untouched. The Great Nightmare had destroyed most of the city, but at least it had left this place intact.

Under the darkness of night, Adonis soared down to the abandoned streets. An eerie silence had fallen over the city.

Flying through the shadows, we touched down behind the abandoned Jewel Tower—across the street from the cathedral.

Adonis lowered me to the ground, then leaned in to whisper in my ear. "Don't let me lose track of you again."

He traced his fingertips over my shoulder, right in the place where he'd marked me with the *theta*, and warmth spread through my body.

I cupped his face in my hands. "They're just human. It will be fine."

"I'll come back for you when I hear your call." Adonis turned, and the shadows around him seemed to absorb him as he walked away.

An oppressive silence hung over the city, and a shiver danced up my neck. For a thousand years, these streets were teeming with life. Now, it felt like an empty carapace.

I climbed up an old set of stairs until I reached the street. There, across from me, stood the ancient cathedral, where kings and queens had been crowned for a thousand years. Iridescent magic glimmered around it, sparkling like a canopy of stars. I felt reassured knowing that the humans here were smart enough to have protected the place—but concerned that they'd done it in such an ostentatious way. I doubted they understood what Metatron was capable of. Magic wouldn't protect them from his power, and a grand display like this would only attract his attention. Given the showiness of the magic, Metatron already knew they were here. He probably just didn't consider them much of a threat.

I surveyed the outside of the cathedral before crossing the road. Two human guards stood in front of the shimmering shield of magic. They clutched semiautomatic rifles.

I smoothed out my hair. I'd taken care with my outfit, hoping to convey "I'm a normal human here."

Before his untimely demise, Elan had left behind a multitude of cat sweatshirts. I'd chosen to wear one that depicted a cat eating pizza and tacos in front of a starry sky. I'd even painted my nails with chipped nail polish, just like a human would.

When you had to meet with people who might kill you, it helped to let them underestimate you. Plus, I knew enough about the human race to understand that they loved weird cat stuff. Just like anything else, this was a performance, and I had to dress the part. Except unlike with my burlesque shows, this performance had life-or-death consequences.

As soon as the guards saw me moving through the darkness, their bodies stiffened, rifles pointed at me.

"Don't you fucking move!" one of them shouted, spittle flying from his mouth.

Gods below. I guess I still conveyed some sense of threat even in the stupid cat sweatshirt.

I held up my hands, showing them I had no weapons. "Easy does it, gentlemen. The Council is expecting me." That's what the humans had started calling themselves. *The Council.*

One of the humans—a stocky fellow who looked like a squashed Chuck Norris—stepped forward. "What's the secret password?"

I sighed. I'd forgotten about the password. Or perhaps I'd temporarily repressed it. "Cock-arsing bollocks," I mumbled.

"What?"

"Cock-arsing bollocks," I said a little louder. Real mature, these guys.

Stocky Chuck Norris nodded, then shouted into the air, "Fuck-stick patrol!"

The magic shimmered away, and a large wooden door behind him groaned open.

❧ 17 ❧

"**N**ow," he barked. "Before we put the shield back up."

I hurried past them, moving quickly into the transept.

The city hadn't had electricity in months, but candles had been lit in sconces and chandeliers around the cathedral. Light danced over the ivory flagstones in Poets' Corner, where Chaucer, Spenser, and Tennyson had been buried centuries ago.

So here we were. The poets and thinkers who represented humanity's greatest gifts to the world, guarded by men who shouted *Fuck-stick patrol* at each other.

My footsteps echoed off the high ceiling as I walked farther into the ancient space. There, on the ornate mosaic floor and among the gilt candleholders of Westminster's altar, stood three women. I searched in the shadows, but I didn't see Alex.

I raised a hand in greeting. "I'm Ruby."

The first person to step forward was a curvy young woman with shoulder-length hair, dressed in a Mickey Mouse

T-shirt. Already, I was feeling confident about my taco-cat clothing choice.

"Lila here," she said. "Girl, they made you use bullshit passwords, didn't they?"

I nodded. "Cock-arsing bollocks."

"Charming." A second leader stepped forward—one with dewy skin and smooth, auburn hair. "You're Ruby, I take it. I'm Amber."

"I'm Brianna," said the last one—a young woman with a chin-length blond bob.

"We put those men in charge of security so they feel important," said Brianna. "Stops them from trying to make crucial decisions, but they get to choose the passwords."

I frowned. "Speaking of men, I thought Alex was supposed to be here."

Lila stepped closer to me, looking me up and down carefully. "Alex! Is this her?" she shouted into the shadows.

Alex stepped into the candlelight, a smile lighting up his face. "That's most definitely Ruby."

He looked even leaner than the last time I saw him, a ragged sweater hanging off his thin frame. I ran over to him, throwing my arms around his neck in a hug. "Alex! I missed you. Sorry about disappearing. And about pointing an arrow at you."

I pulled away from Alex, meeting the blonde's gaze. "So how did you three get to be leaders?"

"Each of us represents a faction of the resistance from different territories," said Brianna.

Lila shoved her hands in her pockets, eying me warily. "Probably best if we don't give too much information."

Pretty suspicious for a girl in a Mickey Mouse T-shirt.

I nodded at the exit. "I take it by the ostentatious display of magic that you're not too worried about the angels discovering your location."

Amber flicked her auburn hair over her shoulder. "We've got some of the world's best mages working with us. We want the angels to see what kind of power we have. The essence of Devil's Bane imbues that force field. If any angels touch it, their bodies will dissolve like ice in a lava flow."

This might be my chance to provide them with some valuable information so they'd know I was on their side. "Yeah, that's not going to stop Metatron."

"Who?" asked Lila.

"Leader of the Heavenly Host, father of the horsemen, all around terrifying fuck-stick of an angel. To use your guard's term. He's been keeping the Heavenly Host in hiding and slowly transforming them into immortal beings. From what I understand, he is the most adept speaker of the Angelic language in the universe. I think he can break your shield. I think he can break everything."

Brianna's face paled. Then, she straightened. "In the worst-case scenario, the mages can transport us to one of the magical realms. The angels won't find us."

Lila folded her arms in front of her cartoon shirt. I wouldn't say the look on her face was exactly welcoming. "We're not transporting anywhere. This—London—is our home. They've invaded, and we're fighting back to protect us. You've been living with the angels. You really want us to trust you?" She moved closer to me, her shoes clacking off the floor.

"She's been working with the Institute," said Alex. "She's been undercover among the horsemen, gathering information, even before the resistance was formed."

Lila's jaw tightened. "I know that. But now she's working with the Hunter. Isn't that right? You want us to join an alliance with two of the horsemen who've been slaughtering us." Tears shone in her eyes, and her cheeks turned pink. "I watched one of my friends torn to pieces in the streets by his hounds." She pulled up the sleeve of her sweatshirt, displaying a brutal scar where some of the flesh had been torn off her arm. "His hounds did this to me."

Oh, balls.

I had known this was going to be a hard sell, and the taco cat on my sweatshirt might not be enough to smooth it over. But I didn't think it would be "watched my friend eaten by dogs" bad. Or "he ripped the flesh off my arms" bad.

I took a deep breath. I wanted to say that Kratos couldn't control it—that he'd been cursed by Metatron and forced to hunt. But this would just sound like a bunch of bullshit excuses to them. They'd never feel sympathy for him or care why he'd done it.

I had to appeal to something more powerful. A desperate will to live. "Yes, Kratos—the Hunter—is part of the alliance I want you to join. As I'm sure you know, he is no longer hunting humans. The simple fact is, a war has erupted between the horsemen. Two of the horsemen are trying to end life on earth as we know it. They want to kill all of us and start fresh. They want to create a race of humans born only to worship them and Metatron. The two horsemen who oppose them are willing to wage war against them, and we need to work with them. Because guess who's not going to win a war against immortal angels? Humans."

Alex frowned. "You think humans are weak against the angels, and maybe we are. So why are you so eager to form an alliance with us?"

And here's where my pitch got *really* difficult. "To give us the greatest chance of winning, we might need you to change a bit."

Amber furrowed her brow. "Change us? What are you talking about?"

"Look, I'm just going to lay it out for you," I said. "Right now, your chances of survival are not good. Metatron can get through your shields and slaughter you all within seconds."

"Even if that's true," said Brianna doubtfully, "How exactly are you proposing that we change?"

"We can make you more durable."

"Bollocks," said Lila. "How?"

"You'd have to stop being human."

"What are you on about?" snapped Lila.

"There's a way to convert you to demons and fae," I said. "Whatever species you choose. You'd have magic, maybe the ability to fly. As a demon, you could be immortal. As a fae, your life would extend for centuries."

"You've got to be bloody joking," said Lila.

"I definitely didn't come here to tell jokes."

"First," said Brianna, "you want us to accept the Hunter as an ally. Now you want us to transform into the demons who have been attacking us since the Great Nightmare began."

This wasn't going well. "You'd still be you. Just more powerful. And more importantly, you'll be alive." I sighed. "Look, I'm not human, but I lived among you. Just like you, I watched my loved ones taken from me. The day angels came to earth, I watched a dragon shifter kill my boyfriend in front of my eyes. I watched my sister taken from me while Kratos flew through the skies above us."

I nodded at Alex.

"Alex and I lived in a rookery in Whitechapel, fighting gangs over rat meat, just like you've been doing. I remember the Hunter coming through the city at night. I remember trembling in fear when I heard his hounds howling. The Great Nightmare changed me. After everything I'd seen, I started getting scared of the dark. I slept in a windowless room, hiding my candle from the others because I couldn't face the shadows. This is our chance to come out into the light again. This is our chance to rebuild. You have two options. You can stay human and die, or you can adapt and survive. You're leaders. Lead. Your job is to make sure your people survive at all costs."

Amber shot me a fierce look. "Demons have done nothing on earth except feed from us. Humans have created everything you see here." She gestured at Poets' Corner. "Shakespeare, Darwin, Byron—all human. Galileo, Newton, Einstein —all human. We are earth's actors, its creators. We built civilization, and we're here to defend it. And now you want us to give all that up and become monsters? Leeches? What exactly are we defending if we become like them? We were born human, and we're meant to stay human."

"You can protect the other humans by adapting." I shook my head. "Clinging too hard to what you believe is your nature is dangerous. It's a shackle around your throat. Sometimes I'm a fae, sometimes a human. Sometimes I'm a succubus. None of these things are my destiny. We all have to adapt to survive, and the fact is, if you don't form an allegiance with us, human culture won't survive at all. No more poems, sculptures, or cathedrals. All this turns to ash. No more nursery rhymes or tacos or cat sweatshirts. Just a wasteland populated by human slaves created to worship the horsemen. Do you understand what I'm saying? You can either join us, or die. *Everything* dies."

Join or die. I think I'd seen that slogan on some old human propaganda, and it seemed like it might be effective. In fact, it seemed perhaps like the perfect note to end on.

I turned, crossing to the cathedral's doors. I'd done my job for now—planting a seed of an idea in their minds. They didn't seem like they were jumping at the chance to become a mob of vampires and ogres, and I didn't blame them. But surely they'd spent enough time scrambling for rat meat and dying from dysentery to know that death lingered for them around every corner.

I pushed open the enormous transept door into the cold night air, and the two guards nodded at me. I crossed into the shadowy street in front of Westminster, heading for my meeting spot with Adonis.

But as I moved closer to the old stairwell, Angelic words began to boom around me, clattering inside my skull until I couldn't hear my own thoughts. Words and fragments appeared and popped in my mind like bubbles.... *Pavem— blood—Marc—fera—drago—beast—*

I fell to the ground, my hands over my ears, trying to block it out. Through the chaos, one idea rang clearly.

Metatron is near.

And in the next moment, my world went black and silent as a grave.

18

I woke in a tiny stone room, hanging from the ceiling in iron manacles, agony burning through my arms. Only the tips of my toes touched the slimy floor.

I knew my manacles were iron by the fact that they sent a deep, throbbing pain racing through my bones, from the wrists down through my shoulders. Also from the fact that my body felt completely drained of all energy, as if someone had sucked all the blood out of me.

I strained, trying to see around me. In the gloom, I couldn't see much beyond the slick stones. The air around me smelled damp and fusty, like old moss. Or like an old fae. As my eyes adjusted, I peered through an arched doorway. Through it, I could vaguely see a spiral staircase leading up to another floor. All I really knew was that I was hanging by my wrists in a vaulted room. Heavy shadows cloaked much of the space.

Something fluttered in the darkness, then burst into the air, cawing. My body tensed until I realized it was just a raven.

A wild guess told me I was in one of the old dungeons at the Tower. And also that I was pretty much screwed. With iron sapping my power and no one to hear me scream in a torture dungeon, it was looking a little bleak. Fear began to crawl up my spine.

If I needed to, I'd call to Adonis through our bond. But I wasn't going to panic just yet. I wanted to know exactly what my enemies had planned here before I called Adonis into the fray. For all I knew, this could be a trap.

Then—from the shadows—*he* appeared. Metatron glowed with pale light. His features looked so much like Adonis's, but he had that otherworldliness about him that disturbed me. He wore his dark hair longer, and it hung over his shoulders, melding with the shadows. His body seemed fuzzy, like I was looking at it through a Vaseline-smeared lens. I didn't quite have a sense of what he was wearing—just an ethereal, white glow around his body.

"Ruby." His voice knelled like a funeral bell. "The great savior. Are those little rocks in your head supposed to ward us all away?"

An uneven stream of water droplets dripped onto me from the ceiling, plunging onto my shoulder, cold and slimy. *Drip, drip ... drip.*

Faintly, the stones tingled. But with the iron digging into my skin, I couldn't summon any of their magic.

An icy wind rippled over me, and I shivered. It was only at this point that I realized I'd been strung up completely naked. "I was actually growing fond of that cat sweatshirt, you know. You fucking pervert."

"Oh, you misunderstand, little beast. I find you physically repulsive."

I narrowed my eyes at him. From what I could tell, he was telling the truth. He looked at my body with all the excitement of a high school student staring at a math problem about train velocity.

"Of course I find you repulsive," he continued. "It's just

that beasts weren't meant to wear clothes. Humans certainly weren't. Don't you know the story of the Garden of Eden?"

The manacles were biting into my flesh, but I tried to keep myself from grunting, or from giving him the pleasure of hearing me struggle. "Yeah, I've heard of it once or twice."

"Humans—beasts like yourself—became self-conscious. They learned they would die someday, that the consciousness they came to think of as eternal would cease to exist. It pained their simple minds. That was their punishment for hubris. They thought of themselves as angels. They weren't."

"Okay. So you're not into human or fae bodies. Good to know." I grimaced at the pain in my arms. "You do realize that I'm not a human, though, right?"

He sniffed the air. "You have a particularly strong fae smell. You smell of moss and dirt. Eons ago, your kind were angels. You chose to live as beasts here on earth. Fighting and fucking like animals. You are worse than humans. Have you ever seen a dog dressed in a suit? That's what you look like to me in your clothing."

"Yes, I get it. Shall we move on? I assume you have a point to all this."

Whatever it took, I needed to get out of these manacles. I just had no idea how. I craned my head, glancing behind me to find a sort of ladder. That was the rack, I thought. If I had to guess, they probably planned to tie me to that at some point for a bit of enhanced interrogations.

His lip twitched in a smile. "I understand you know Aereus."

Footfalls echoed out, and the Horseman of War stepped into the dim light. In his eyes, I didn't find the bland dispassion that Metatron displayed. Nope, Aereus was looking at me like I was a stripper at his prison release party.

This all just got more fun. "Did you know that your lovely son here has a prurient interest in animals?"

Metatron ignored me, taking another step closer. "It was the worst mistake an angel ever made—giving divine knowledge to the animals. I listened in on your little meeting in the cathedral. Very interesting. The humans are quite proud of their scientists and their poets. They don't commemorate the truth. Shall I show you what they leave out of Poets' Corner? The real work of humans. Their singular ability to devise creative ways to torture, maim, and kill. Everything we're going to do to you here in this prison was designed by humans. Remember that."

Oh, this didn't sound good. In fact, my mouth was starting to go dry, and I really wanted to puke.

The pain in my wrists was starting to take my breath away. "You have a very selective interpretation of history."

"Humans were given the gift of language, of magic," said Metatron. "And what did they do with it? They squandered it. Do you know that war and violence are the primary drivers of human technology and advancement? You all could have used their gifts for working with each other, but you didn't. That's why we need to burn it all and start again."

Metatron spoke a few words in Angelic, and a vision rose before my eyes.

A thin, blond woman lay strapped to a rack, dressed in only a tiny white dress. Two men flanked the rack, one of them with his meaty fists on a wooden wheel at her feet. When he began turning the wheel, her face contorted with pain. She appeared to shriek, then she lost consciousness.

"Anne Askew," said Metatron. "Tortured nearly to death, right here in the Tower. And for what? Some differences in theology that none of them were right about in the first place. They turned the handles so hard, that they ripped dear old Anne apart. They dislocated her elbows and knees, pulled all her joints out of their sockets. She screamed so loud they heard her outside the Tower walls. And when they finished, they carried her broken body to Smithfield—the meat market —where they burned her alive."

Bile rose in my throat, and I closed my eyes. I didn't want to see it, didn't want to hear it. I wanted to run back to the humans to listen to them talk about Darwin again. Still, I needed to keep him stalling, at least long enough until I could think of a plan.

The vision disappeared with a flick of Metatron's hand. "I know what's in your soul, little animal. I can see it smudged on your forehead like a bloodstain. You dream of a simple life in a cottage. Like that fae couple you saw."

I swallowed hard. His ability to see into my mind both-ered the hell out of me. I didn't mind him looking at my naked body, but reading my thoughts felt like a complete violation. "Is there a point to all this?" I snapped.

Aereus grinned. "We just want to break your mind before we break your body."

My gut churned. *Think of a plan, Ruby, think of a plan.*

"Pathetic, really," said Metatron. "Your dream of a fae utopia in the woods. You and my son. Do you really think he belongs with a creature like you? Eating soup?"

I didn't answer. His intrusion enraged me.

"He doesn't even like soup," Metatron continued.

"It's not about the soup!" I shouted. *Who doesn't like soup? It's so weird.*

"Would you like to see more from your little fae friends?" Metatron asked.

"No," I replied. "Not at all, actually."

"Too bad."

From the darkness, a second vision arose. It was that cottage I'd seen in the woods. An emaciated fae boy was walking toward it, his features gaunt. He knocked on the door, and the woman opened it.

The woman smiled, her cheeks dimpling. Then, she

lunged for the boy. Her teeth were in his neck before he knew what hit him, blood pouring from his throat.

My heart clenched. Adonis had said he'd smelled blood when we passed that place.

My lip curled. "I get it. You don't like anyone who's not an angel."

After everything Metatron had showed me in here, part of me was starting to wonder if he was right. The smartest species on earth were also the most brutally sadistic. Beasts with the minds of angels—a dangerous combination. What if I'd been viewing everything through rose-tinted glasses, romanticizing a life that just didn't exist? Humans who used science to kill, fae who ate their own.

Maybe Adonis was right, and we were all slaves to our own natures.

He is Death; I am a beast, and all of us were born to hurt each other.

19

"You must understand now." Metatron steepled his fingertips. "This is why it's time for a reckoning. If humans had worshipped me like they were supposed to in the first place, if they'd remained humble, none of us would be here. But they desired supremacy over each other, the way gods like me are supposed to reign supreme over the beasts." Metatron cocked his head. "Strange to me that all those people like dear old Anne allowed themselves to be tortured because of moderately different interpretations of religious texts. You were meant to worship me. You all got it wrong. What would you die for, Ruby? Shall we find out?"

One thing, and one thing alone: the people I love.

"Ahh. You'd die for my son. How sweet."

He was listening in on my thoughts again, and I wanted to rip his smug, glowing face off.

He moved closer to me, his eyes curious now. "Maybe torturing you isn't the worst thing, then. Maybe watching your loved ones die painful deaths would be worse."

I swallowed hard. "Would you kill your own son?"

"I can't kill him. Only you can do that. But if I hurt you enough, you'll give in. Beasts like you will always save themselves in the end, even if you make yourselves weak with your attachments. Love weakens you, just like the iron does. Because when you turn on Adonis, it will break you completely."

I shuddered. Metatron was a complete monster.

Faint light glinted off Aereus's armor, and he took a step forward. "Adonis will come for you, of course. We'll make you kill him. Then you die. Then the rest of the world. In just three days, my army of immortals will begin rampaging through one city after another. They will cleanse the world of the rest of the humans and demons who hid like rats in the sewers. Busy week, honestly."

Panic slammed me in the gut. In three days? We only had three days before everyone and everything died. Still, I tried to think clearly. If I managed to get out of here alive, this was my opportunity to gather some intelligence from them. I needed to know what their exact plan was.

What was the best way to get people to tell you things when they had all the power? Naked and chained to the ceiling, I couldn't exactly scare him into giving me information. I had to appeal to his weaknesses. Unfortunately, he didn't seem to have any, except for the fact that he was really hung up on the "worship me" thing.

"When you attack, people all over the world will tremble before you," I said, looking straight at Metatron. "Everyone will know your name."

He stared at me. Maybe that was a little too much. I needed him talking, not gaping at me.

Let me try that again. "I beg you to rethink this. As you march from one city to another, the people who remain will know the true meaning of fear and terror. Their last remaining moments on earth will be filled with thoughts of you instead of thoughts of their loved ones. I beseech you to change your mind."

The white light intensified around him. "They should think about me. I don't see what the problem is there."

I let my eyes go wider. "Can you picture it, Metatron? Can you picture the destruction, the fear?"

"We will make humans bleed from their ears," Aereus cut in, his face reddening. "From their chests and throats."

Metatron shot Aereus an irritated look, like a father who wanted his son to stop showing off at the dinner table. "The important thing isn't that as we kill, humans will know the true meaning of divine perfection through my presence. If they don't know it through worship, they will know it through my wrath."

What. An. Asshole.

"Of course!" I simpered. "Your divine power is overwhelming. I can feel it changing me already. Inspiring me with divine grace."

I closed my eyes, thinking of some kind of ecstatic state. "So amazing to be in the presence of a real god. I can imagine you moving first through the City of London, inspiring sacred terror. In fact, I'm having a vision. A divinely inspired vision. First, you'll move through Westminster, then you spread through the rest of London, then Kent...."

"I'm bored of hearing you speak," said Metatron. "And I have someone else I'd like you to meet."

With that, he turned and slipped into the darkness of the hallway.

Shit. That line of interrogation had gotten me nowhere, and I had a feeling he was about to introduce someone even more unpleasant to my afternoon.

Aereus stared at me, licking his lips. He took a few steps closer. "You think you're so smart. Bollocks. We're not even going the way you said. We start in East London, then we move up to Northamptonshire. Spread through the North, then Denmark, and on to the rest of Europe."

Okay, so forget about appealing to someone's ego. Maybe the best strategy was always "get the dumbest person in the room to tell you stuff."

"When?" I asked.

"We leave at dawn, three days from now. That's all the time you have left until all your human friends die."

In all likelihood, Aereus didn't see me as a threat, anyway. He probably didn't expect me to make it out of here alive at all.

My mouth went dry as I waited to see who Metatron was about to bring back. My torturer, I assumed. At this point, I was glad I hadn't told Adonis where I was. This was all part of a trap to lure him here, so they could try to torture me into killing him.

Would I break?

My throat tightened, and raw fear snaked over my skin. I must have let some of that fear slip through the bond, because for the first time, I felt something coming through the bond toward me. Not words, but a feeling. Adonis's fear, mirroring my own.

Footsteps echoed in the corridor outside, and then Metatron returned through the arched doorway. By his side was a squat man wielding a dull-looking axe.

Yep, this was about to get a whole lot worse.

Metatron stepped closer, his face still wearing a bored expression. "If Adonis doesn't come on his own, we'll have to entice him a bit. He can feel your emotions, can't he? Let's give him something to really feel."

Dried blood coated the blade. The man wore a shabby tunic that looked like it belonged to another century.

Metatron gestured to him. "May I introduce Jack Ketch, the most sadistic executioner in England's history. I revived him, just for this. I hope you appreciate the effort I went through. I'll leave you alone to his ministrations. As he cuts into your flesh, think about whether or not humans like him have made good use of their divine knowledge, or if Azazeyl should have left them as wordless beasts rutting in the shrubs."

Jack flashed me another crooked grin, giving me the distinct impression that he was a snaggle-toothed simpleton with no idea what the hell Metatron was talking about.

Aereus rubbed his hands together. "Perhaps I can help."

Metatron glared at him. "You enjoy it too much. You're at risk of falling. Enjoying sadistic acts is what beasts do. Come."

Aereus scowled, then followed his father through the doorway.

Jack gripped his axe, grinning to reveal rotten teeth. "Collar day for you, pretty thing. Oooh, but I'd love to flog you at the cart's arse."

No idea what he meant, but the creepiness came through just fine. If this was who Metatron spent time around, no wonder he hated humans.

My heart began to race. I tried to slow it, worried I'd draw Adonis here with the fear blazing through our bond. Once Adonis arrived, my torments would probably only get worse.

I surveyed the room again, now that my eyes had adjusted, and caught a glimpse of the dark leaves crawling around the stone walls. *Devil's Bane.* That's how they planned to subdue Adonis while they tortured me. Adrenaline sparked through my nerves, electrifying me.

Gods below. If I could only get out of the handcuffs, I could control the plants completely. Maybe I could even kill these fuckers. My gaze flicked upward, where the iron bit into my wrists. How the hell could I get this off me?

Jack grinned, staring at my thighs. "I'll start with your pretty shanks...."

Stupid of Metatron to leave me here alone, but maybe he had a hard time believing a tiny chick wearing a taco-cat sweatshirt could fuck anyone up. *Always let your enemy underestimate you.*

I widened my eyes and bit my lip. "Jack, you have such a fearsome reputation. I don't think I can ... I don't think I can take it...." I let my head loll to the side, as if I'd just fainted.

Whatever time period he was from, women probably fainted all the time. Maybe this unrealistic performance wasn't much of a stretch.

"Ooooh, you dimber wench," he burbled. "I'd like to get my nimble fingers on your crinkum crankum before I cut you open."

What. The. Fuck.

Through a slit in my eyes, I watched him lay down his axe. When he reached for me, I swung my legs, tightening them around his neck. I squeezed hard, trying to block out the unfortunate proximity of his face to my *crinkum crankum.*

I snapped his neck. Humans were such fragile things.

Jack fell to the ground—dead once more, like he was supposed to be.

Now, I needed to get out of the damn manacles. I had very thin wrists, and if I had something to lubricate them a bit, I could probably slide them out....

Drip, drip ... drip.

Right. The ceiling slime.

I swung my body back just a little until I caught a rung with my toes. I scrambled back onto the ladder until my heels were resting on a rung. From there, I stepped my way up the ladder until the chains were slack, and I could reach the ceiling with my manacles. I began rubbing them against the dungeon slime—a sort of mixture of water, moss, and gods-knew-what—until it covered the iron completely. Then, I yanked the chains down to my foot, and used it to put pressure on the links between the manacles. Grimacing, I pressed hard on the chain, and the iron scraped against my wrists. With the help of the slime, I was able to scrape them down to my hands, though it took some skin off with it. Already, I could feel the iron poisoning my blood, and I wanted to puke.

From somewhere above, Metatron's voice was booming off the stones. *He's coming back.*

My heart slammed against my ribs as I caught a glimpse of his pearly glow on the stairwell. *He's going to kill me.*

Then—at last—I slid the manacles off, and magic surged through my bones. The gemstones in my forehead began to heat up, and I let my mind merge with the plants around me. Their spirits called to me, and I felt as if they were my children. I beckoned them closer, and the ropes of Devil's Bane began peeling off the wall, sliding across the floor toward me, until the vines had wrapped themselves around my body like a makeshift dress.

In the next moment, Metatron was standing before me, with Aereus close behind. Light beamed from my body, creating a sort of shield, exploding from the inside out. The magic of the Old Gods surged in my skull, but his words were confusing me, creating chaos until I could no longer remember what I was supposed to be doing....

As he spoke, rock and stone rained from the ceiling, slamming against the shield I'd created, threatening to smash through it.

Fight the angel ... magical myster ... longitu ... apple clipper sternum malc drip....

I clamped my hands over my ears, trying to drown out the noise so I could fight him. *He's going to kill ... he's ... kill ... shrill mockingbir ... oyster....*

Ravens burst out of the shadows, fluttering around me,

and their caws echoed off the stone walls, drowning out the sounds of Angelic. Then, darkness crept in like a miasma. The shadows had a heaviness to them, vast and overwhelming, a disorienting void that sucked up everything around it—even my own light—until I could see only blackness. And with it—sweet, merciful silence.

Once, darkness terrified me beyond measure. Once, I'd slept with a candle burning by my bed all night. Now, by the soothing tinge of the darkness, I knew Adonis had come.

With the Angelic language dulled, I could focus on my plant magic again. In the darkness, I sent my vines out, searching for my enemies. Through my connection to the vines, I felt them wrap around Metatron and Aereus, squeezing them tighter. Then, Metatron launched into another of his spells, and I could feel the vines crumbling. My body ached as they fell to pieces—but along with their demise, the walls were crumbling around us too, debris raining down on us. Chaos, of course, was hard to control.

Before Metatron had a chance to utter another spell, I felt Adonis's arms around me. He curled his body around mine protectively. Then, we were zooming through the air at the speed of a tornado wind.

Stone shattered around us, and I shielded my head with my arms.

Adonis had burst through the rock walls to free us, and blood streaked his face as we soared into the London sky.

❧ 2 0 ❧

In the forest outside Hotemet Castle, I walked between the oaks, my bow slung over my back. With each step, a dull pain shot up my legs. The iron from the manacles still poisoned my system.

I'd spent the past hour out here, practicing my magic. But each time I used a more powerful spell, I felt the Old Gods overwhelming me until I was certain I'd lose my mind.

Now, a cold wind whispered through the trees, skimming my bare legs and making me shiver. Clouds roiled in the sky, the color of iron, and the sun had begun to set.

Today, I wasn't quite as in love with nature. Since my escape from the Tower earlier, the forest didn't seem to hold the beauty that it once had. Particularly since I'd already happened upon a large blackbird eating a baby blackbird that writhed in the dirt, its body malformed. I was never one for superstitions, but that had to be a bad omen, right? It was the kind of image Aereus would have framed and stuck on his wall.

And yet the destructiveness of nature seemed like it was all around me now. Crushed acorns littered the ground—little seedlings that had never made it into trees, each one of them a failed life. What if Eden had only been a paradise because humans were too dumb to see the decay around them, just like I'd been?

Every living thing in this forest would die at some point. In the end, chaos ruled everything, and sometimes the old ate the young.

So that was the kind of mood I was in.

As I walked through an alder grove, a familiar soothing magic whispered over my body, tinged with myrrh. All it took was the scent of Adonis to heat my blood, and I'd moved on from *death whispers all around us* to *let's get naked in a bath again.* Even though, technically, he *was* Death.

I turned to find him walking toward me, a faint smile curling his sensual lips. Dark, finely cut clothes accentuated his perfect body, and he wore a sword slung over his back. "What are you doing brooding out here? Don't you know that's my job?"

"Just wondering if I've been wrong about nature and paradise and all that crap. And maybe the forest is a cemetery, where a seed of death lies within every berry and fern and apple tree. That kind of fun stuff."

"You definitely sound like me. Have I gotten into your head?" He looked mesmerized as he gazed at me, and he closed the distance between us. Then, he stroked the back of his knuckles down my cheek. "No. Metatron got in your head, didn't he?"

"Your dad is an asshole."

"I could have told you that." His pale eyes shone like beacons in the forest's gloom. "But death gives rise to new life, doesn't it? Plants grow from the soil fertilized by the dead. It's not an endpoint. It's just part of a cycle."

One last ray of sunlight broke free from the clouds, gilding the perfect planes of his face. Already, his presence was soothing me, his otherworldly beauty an antidote to the ugliness of nature. "I think I have an idea of how to convince the humans to join us."

He arched a perfect eyebrow. "How, exactly?"

"Metatron showed me images of people being tortured. I always knew it was something that happened in the world, something that humans did. But seeing it right before my eyes disturbed me on another level. What if I gave the humans a clear visual image of what they were facing?"

"Facing death, you mean?"

"The deaths of people they love. Metatron said that love makes us weak, but only if you define strength as an unyielding stubbornness. I saw a vision of a woman who died for an idea. Something theological. I'd die only to protect those I love, and so would most people. Love can give us strength, can push us to make the right choices: the will to survive, to protect those we care about. The strength to adapt when we need to. Life is too precious to waste on ideals like staying human just for the sake of it."

"You want to remind them that they're fighting for those they love."

"Exactly. What if I used my powers of illusion to convince humans? They need to see firsthand what can happen to their loved ones if they don't join us."

"Terrify them into compliance. I like your tactics."

"They need to understand that people's children will die if they don't join us."

"There's a little problem with your plan."

"Oh?"

"The entire resistance has disappeared."

I blinked. "Disappeared?"

"Yasmin has just told us. It seems there were mages among them."

"Yeah. They were very proud of their mages. The best

mages in the world, apparently. But they didn't know what we know. We only have three days before everything ends."

Adonis cocked his head. "And, unfortunately, I think they might have overestimated their mages' abilities."

A chill snaked up my neck. "What happened, exactly?

"After you told them Metatron could get through their shields, they panicked. When a king from another realm offered them asylum in his kingdom, they jumped at the chance. He's supposedly offering them space in his castle."

"Why did they leave so fast?"

"They thought they could plan the resistance from there, unperturbed by the angels. They transported the entire army to a magical realm. Only one old woman stayed behind, unwilling to jump into an unknown kingdom. She didn't want to risk the journey. It seems they didn't leave time to research the realm, and they might have jumped somewhere completely inhospitable."

My stomach clenched. Alex was among them. Was he in trouble? "Do you have any idea how to find them?"

"I've found them through scrying, and I can get us there. I don't know much beyond the location, but I can open a portal in and out."

"You're sure you can get them out?"

He looked affronted. "Of course I can, Ruby. I'm more powerful than their idiot human mages."

"Let's go, then. Now. I've got my bow and arrow, and I'm ready to shoot things if I need to."

Adonis grabbed me by the hand, pulling me toward the river. The sun had now dipped lower behind the trees, and I shivered in the cooling air. Once we reached the river, Adonis pulled me toward the edge. The water flowed fast, shimmering like quicksilver in the darkening forest.

"Are you ready for a swim?"

Goosebumps covered my skin beneath my dress. It felt a

little cold to jump in the river, but with Metatron on the verge of unleashing his army of immortals, time was running short.

As we stood at the edge of the river, Adonis spoke in Angelic, and his powerful magic rippled over my body, electrifying me. I stared at the river as its churning waters grew darker. Then, a few sparks of electricity ignited on its surface.

"Could this realm be dangerous?" I asked.

"Yes, but we can leave through a portal any time we need to."

Holding each other's hands, we jumped into the river. Icy water enveloped our bodies.

Underwater, Adonis pulled me close to his powerful chest, and warmth radiated from his body as we sank deeper below the surface. My lungs began to burn the deeper we went down.

In the water's darkness, eels swam around us, their bodies blazing with electric pulses. That was eerie. I was starting to have a very bad feeling about this location.

At last, Adonis tugged my hand, and we began swimming for the surface. We reached the top, and I gasped for air, resting my elbows on the lip of a stone basin. I caught my breath for a moment, heaving air into my lungs. Then, I hoisted myself out, flopping to the cobblestones below like a dying fish.

My dress was completely soaked, and my teeth began to chatter as I looked around me. We were standing on a stone lane of a ramshackle old city. Rickety timber-frame buildings crowded the roads, their surfaces covered in thorny branches and—disconcertingly—Devil's Bane.

We'd just arrived through a drinking fountain that featured a gorgon spewing water. At the top of a stone obelisk in the fountain, an enormous copper spike speared the sky. Dark clouds roiled above us, and I shivered.

Here, night was falling quickly. I wasn't as scared of the dark as I'd once been—not since I'd stolen the power of the Old Gods. Still, this place gave me the heebie-jeebies. I shivered, relieved that I'd brought my bow and arrow with me.

From our spot in the town square, the street snaked up a hill. And on top of the hill itself stood a dark, tottering castle. Between its spindly copper spires, electricity sparked rhythmically, like a heartbeat.

I glanced at Adonis. On the journey here, he'd hidden his wings. He didn't look particularly concerned about our current situation, but then, he rarely did.

He narrowed his gray eyes. "Whoever rules this place has covered it in Devil's Bane. Maybe the king has heard about the Great Nightmare even from within his sealed-off realm. He certainly doesn't want angels or horsemen here."

A tavern sign creaked in the wind, its chipped surface reading *Adam & Lucifer,* with an image of a painted snake.

A man and a woman burst from the pub, slamming the wooden door open and tumbling into the street. The woman's lips were painted red, and she wore vibrant skirts with a tight black bustier. Another woman followed behind her, breasts spilling out of her gown. No one could say that this realm lacked for cleavage.

Still, something looked *off* about them—their movements a little jerky, eyes a little haunted.

Thunder boomed, and a spear of lightning cracked the sky, touching down on the copper post to our right. I jumped, practically leaping on Adonis before recovering myself.

His lip curled in a wry smile. "A little scared of lightning, are we?"

I scowled at him. "Don't be ridiculous."

I surveyed the buildings around us once more, the thin chimneys jutting from rooftops like crooked teeth. Copper spikes protruded from some of them, and electricity sparked from their points.

I reached out for the vines covering one of the buildings. "Can this Devil's Bane affect you even if it's not touching you?"

"With this much around me, it's already sapping my powers."

I swallowed hard. Guess we'd be counting on my powers here, although the iron had wrecked me a bit. "Think we're supposed to head up to that castle?"

"That would be my guess. But considering this world is hostile to angels, I think it's best if we walk instead of fly."

Even though the dark buildings around us looked like they were falling apart, a sensual and alluring scent floated on a warm breeze, skimming over my skin.

As we walked, my arm brushed against Adonis, and a shiver of pleasure rippled over my body. Here, my mind felt different, my body strangely heated. I glanced at Adonis, whose spine had stiffened.

He slid his gaze to me. "There's an aphrodisiac in the air. Designed to distract us."

Oh, shit. I had a feeling we were in trouble.

❧ 21 ❧

"**R**ight," I breathed. "So, we have electric eels, lightning rods, aphrodisiacs. That all adds up to...."

"Yes?"

"I have no idea, actually. It's all just fucking weird, and I can't think straight."

Thunder rumbled over the horizon again and lightning ignited the sky, touching down on a lightning rod over the palace spires. The skies opened up and rain began hammering down from above.

I felt my nipples harden under my soaking wet dress. As we walked along the winding streets, the hairs stood up on the back of my neck, and I started to have the sense that someone was watching us.

My chest flushed, and I glanced at Adonis again, running my tongue over my lower lip. I couldn't stop thinking about how his body had felt pressed against mine underwater. My heart beat faster, chest and cheeks flushing. *It's only the aphrodisiac, confusing me.*

As we walked, some electric lights cast a flickering glow,

sparking bright white over the tumbledown buildings. We passed another bar—this one called *The Sparking Frog*.

Another woman slammed through the door, this one with platinum curls piled high on her head. She smiled at me, her lips cherry red. Even if she had those same strange, jerky movements, her eyes looked heavy-lidded, a lustful expression on her features. She looked like she'd just been satiated, and I suddenly had a burning desire to feel like that, too. She tottered across the dark road.

I breathed in the exotic scent in the air, feeling as if my breasts were growing heavy and full, and I had the strongest desire to pull Adonis into an alleyway....

I gritted my teeth, trying to stay focused. We were here to find the resistance. My eyes slid to Adonis, roaming over his muscled form. Plenty of time for fucking later.

As if hearing my thoughts, he shot me a wicked smile, and I realized that I'd stopped walking just to stare at him. In fact, I was leaning against a ramshackle wall—a pub, maybe. My bow was pushing into my back, annoying me. It didn't matter. What mattered was that heat pulsed between my legs, and my body ached for Adonis's touch. I tugged up the hem of my dress, and Adonis's gaze devoured every inch of my exposed thighs.

"Adonis," I said. My legs trembled, and I yearned for him —for his dark power.

I clenched my fists, trying to remember what we were doing here.

The resistance. Resist. Resist.

"Plenty of time for fucking later," I managed, even as his possessive hands were grabbing my hips. My arms found their way around his neck, and I pulled him closer. "Plenty of time for your mouth on my breasts, for me to rub against you, touching you everywhere...."

What was I talking about?

His hot mouth found its way to my neck, and he murmured against it. "I could hike up your dress and take you right here if you wanted."

Oh, gods, I wanted that more than I'd ever wanted anything in my life. The raw ache built in me so strongly, liquid heat surging through my body. Adonis's magic spiraled off of him, caressing my skin up my thighs, under my skirt, in all the places I wanted his fingers to reach.

Adonis reached down, grabbing my wrists and pinning them to the wall. My back arched into him. He leaned down, brushing his lips over my throat. I felt my legs widening, and my hips pressed against him. I wanted his mouth to move lower. Instead, he brushed slow kisses up my neck until he locked his gaze on me once more—his gray eyes fierce and hungry. He was a man used to restraining himself. I wanted him to let go, for once to completely give in to pleasure. I wanted his hand to reach the apex of my legs.

His pale eyes pierced me, and I gazed into them help-lessly, mesmerized by him.

I tugged at my wrists to free them, ready to move things faster, but he held me in place, staying in control. This slow-ness felt like pure agony, and I moaned.

"You belong with me," he said. "Do you know that? Life and death belong together."

Whatever. Just put those hands under my skirt and we're good.

Instead, he leaned in, claiming my mouth in a sensual kiss. He pressed his hard body against mine, and I groaned, opening my mouth to him. His tongue swept against mine, and molten heat arced through my blood. I wanted more of him.

Still kissing me, his hands traced down my arms, skim-ming over my breasts, my hips. I shivered, overcome by desire.

My body ached for him. He pulled away from the kiss, his

fingers now on my thighs. He was torturing me with the lightness of his touch, and I gasped, rocking my hips into him.

I felt my breasts straining against the fabric of my sodden dress, and I tugged down the front of it, exposing my lacy pink bra. Adonis growled, kissing my neck again, teeth grazing my throat until the only words I could hear were *ache, need, want....*

"I want you now, Adonis," I whispered.

Maybe if I pulled off my dress and discarded my panties, I could get him to move faster. I could turn my back to him and get him to take me against the wall. I'd always wanted to fuck someone up against a rickety building covered in thorns and Devil's Bane, in the center of a strange town....

Oh, no, wait. Had I? That didn't quite sound right.

"Adonis," I whispered, gripping his hair. "Something's not right."

He hooked his fingers into the top of my panties, tugging them down. *Oh, gods, I need him to touch me.*

"Yeah," he muttered into my neck. "You're wearing too many clothes."

Air caressed my skin as my panties fell to the ground, and my legs opened wider. I started to tug on his belt.

And yet, somewhere in the back of my mind, I knew this wasn't what we were supposed to be doing. The hairs rose on the back of my neck, that feeling of being observed.

"Adonis," I said. "He's watching us."

Resist. Resist.

Adonis's body tensed, and he froze. All at once, his gaze cleared, jaw clenching, and he pulled away from me. He reached over my head, grabbing a thorny branch, and he yanked it from the wall. He clutched it tightly, until blood poured from his fist into the dirt.

Of course. That was how Adonis controlled himself—for

centuries, when pleasure overtook him, he used pain to control it.

The sight of his blood was enough to clear some of the heat from my body, and I took a deep, shuddering breath. Then I leaned down, pulling up my panties again. I looked furtively around me, catching the eye of a woman in a red dress. She winked at me.

Gods below.

Blood dripped from Adonis's palms. "We're going to have to stay focused."

I took a deep, steadying breath. "So this is what it must be like to be a horseman, always trying to resist temptation? How did you manage for all that time?"

As we moved deeper into the city, the buildings started to look more stable, some now made of smooth stone. "Yes. I could have lovers, but I had to keep myself at an emotional distance. You know what can happen if I become emotionally overwhelmed. In the fourteenth century, I had a close friend, once. A siren named Esmerelda who I met on the shores of Sicily. We used to stay up late, studying the stars. She made me laugh with her impersonations of a drunk priest we knew. One night, a sea monster attacked her, and she nearly died. Death washed off me, killing scores of people with a plague."

Even though he was talking about something super morbid, another wave of that aphrodisiac washed over me. "What about Tanit and Kur? You're close to them."

"True, but nothing can kill those two. I don't have to worry."

"So what changed? Why aren't you running from me?"

"I can't. Your allure is a command I have to obey. I don't have a choice in this, any more than the earth can choose to stop orbiting the sun. No more the ocean can stop crashing against the shore. Your body draws me in with an inexorable gravitational pull. My own will has nothing to do with it."

I frowned, not sure if I should be flattered—although I felt the exact same thing for him. "That sounds ... strangely like a prison sentence."

"It's a prison I'll happily inhabit," he said in a voice that was strangely dreamy for Adonis. Clearly, the aphrodisiac was affecting him again, too.

We reached a small park, where willow trees grew among tall grasses. Lightning cracked the sky, illuminating a few women milling around the park. In this part of the city, the women's dresses had become even shorter—just little lacy scraps, with black stockings that stopped mid-thigh, their breasts on display and nipples painted red....

No one would judge us here. We all wanted the same thing.

I breathed in the heavy scent of spring, and my body started to feel full again. We seemed to have drifted off course, and the tall grasses tickled my feet. I'd taken off my shoes at some point. That ache began pooling between my thighs again, and I grabbed Adonis by the shirt, giving in to that gravitational pull. I needed him near me, and the heat in my body was driving me insane. If I could just get rid of this overwhelming desire, we could move on to ... whatever it was we were doing here.

My fingers found their way into Adonis's shirt, exploring his muscled body, and he let out a low growl.

I couldn't remember why he didn't want to give in to me here, why he wouldn't just take me in the grass right now ... there was some reason, but it was stupid, and I could entice him if I just pulled off my dress.

"Ruby," his lips were at my ear, his breath hot against my skin.

"You. Me. Now." My ability to phrase things elegantly

seemed to have disappeared along with my shoes somewhere. Might as well discard the dress with it. I pulled up the hem of my dress, then tossed it into the grass. Lust lit me on fire.

A cool breeze kissed my skin, and Adonis's gaze raked over me, studying every curve. My pulse roared.

At the look he was giving me, raw need surged. I had a vague sense that we were outside somewhere, that people might be watching, and I really should have my dress on. But I couldn't quite stop myself. I kissed him deeply, rubbing against him as I tried to make the aching stop.

Adonis pulled down my bra, covering one of my nipples with his mouth. I hooked my leg around him, trying to draw him in closer to me. He pressed his hard body into me, teeth skimming my nipple. Then, his tongue swirled over it. He wanted me as badly as I wanted him.

My breath hitched in my throat. "Touch my crinkum crankum...."

He pulled away from my breast. "What?"

Shit. Had I said that out loud? I'd just killed the mood. Godsdamn executioner, getting in my head.

I swallowed hard. "I didn't say anything."

In the next moment, he was spinning me around so I faced the tree. His hands found their way into my panties, and he stroked me with such a light touch between my legs that I thought I might lose my mind.

"Adonis," I moaned, rolling my hips, my ass pressing against him.

His breath was hot against my ear. "Tell me you love me."

I'd say anything he wanted right now just to get him to touch me harder. And in any case, it was the truth. I shuddered as he stroked me again, too lightly. I pressed myself against his hand.

"I love you," I whispered.

Lightning cracked again. An adder slithered though the

grass toward me, and I had a vague sense that I needed to get away from it ... something about venom, but....

"Say it louder," Adonis whispered.

As it slithered up my leg, another wave of pleasure rippled through me. This was how Eve had felt in the Garden of Eden, when Azazeyl had tempted her. This was—

That's when the adder sank its fangs into my thigh.

"Ouch!" I shrieked.

Adonis's body stiffened, and he pulled away from me.

I gripped the adder by its neck—if you could say that a snake had a neck—and pulled it off me. Two red droplets bloomed on my thigh.

"That thing is venomous." He ripped it from my hand. In an instant, the snake went limp. Adonis didn't have to expend much effort to kill—it just kind of happened naturally for him.

The place where the adder had bitten me throbbed, and the pain was enough to bring me back down to earth.

"I need to get the venom out," said Adonis. In the next moment, he was on his knees, his head between my legs, his hot mouth on my thigh. His tongue moved expertly over my skin, sucking out the venom. Involuntarily, I felt my thighs clenching around his head, and I threaded my fingers into his hair.

When I'd imagined Adonis's head between my thighs, snake venom hadn't been in the picture, and yet I wasn't going to complain about the feel of his mouth on my skin.

If I could just get these panties off—

But just as I was thinking it, he pulled his head away. A droplet of blood glistened on his lower lip. "That's the venom out."

"Venom?" I blinked.

He stood. "From the adder bite."

"Right. Yes."

Adonis looked dazed, his eyes half-lidded with lust like mine. Then, he straightened, smoothing out his clothes. "We were on our way to the castle." He reached down to the ground, picked up my dress, and handed it to me.

"I know that. I've been thinking about it the whole time."

When lightning speared the sky again, I found that the women weren't quite as I'd imagined them. Their breasts weren't on display. They wore ordinary frocks, hems at their knees. A few men in suits were standing around, pretending to ignore us, even though I knew they'd seen everything.

With my cheeks reddening, I pulled my wet dress over my body, then snatched my weapons off the ground.

Keep it together, Ruby.

22

We just barely managed to keep our clothes on the rest of the way up to the castle.

A long, crooked stone bridge spanned a moat between where we stood and the castle itself. Electric lights flickered inside the narrow castle windows. There were no guards here, no soldiers to protect the place.

"Any idea where we are?"

Adonis shook his head, staring at his palm. Blood still ran from the thorn wounds, pooling on the pavement. "No, but all the Devil's Bane is weakening me. My body isn't even healing like it should."

I swallowed hard. "Maybe this is a bad idea. Maybe I should come back with Hazel, or someone else impervious to the Devil's Bane."

He narrowed his eyes at me. "No way. You are not sending me away for my safety to come back with a teenaged fae."

I could already tell there was no arguing with him. And in any case, we really didn't have much time to lose.

"Let's see if we can get in there, then."

We stood before the castle's entrance, and a pulse of electricity surged between the spires above us. It had a clear rhythm to it, and I guessed there must have been some kinds of thin wires connecting them. Beneath our feet, a sheen of copper glinted from the cobblestones.

This whole city looked like it had been built to conduct electricity.

An eerie feeling rippled over me, and I suddenly felt very grateful for the bow and arrows I'd brought with me. Despite all the aphrodisia, this whole place creeped me out. I stared at the entrance—an ordinary-looking wooden door with what looked like an electric buzzer—wondering if we were just supposed to ring the doorbell. But before I crossed the stones toward it, a shudder whispered up my spine.

Loud, thumping footfalls turned my head, and I whirled to find a monstrous man looming over us. At the sight of his face, my mouth went dry.

He held a torch aloft, and it cast wavering light over his misshapen face. His skin looked piecemeal, like it had been poorly sewn together. It had a yellowish hue, stretched tightly over his bones. It was practically translucent, and I could see the sinews and muscles through it. He must have been at least eight feet tall, dressed in rags, with the dark lips of a corpse....

Suddenly the pieces were starting to come together in my mind. The emptied graves I'd seen in London, the missing corpses, the jerky movements of this city's inhabitants, the electricity everywhere.

"Somewhere in this city is a necromancer," I whispered. "We should be very careful."

Adonis stared at the corpse, his expression unimpressed. "Please don't tell me the festering bag of flesh before us is the king of this place."

Adonis had spent so much time being immortal, and completely immune to any kind of harm, that he really had no idea when to shut up. Even when Devil's Bane had made him vulnerable.

"Not a king," said the corpse.

Honestly, the fact that he could talk—and talk clearly— surprised me.

"Not a king," the creature repeated as he straightened. He pressed a hand to his fleshy chest. "A monster who roams this earth alone, scorned intensely by all who behold me for my wretchedness. Why do I live? I've been cursed with a countenance that inspires dread, and yet deep within my bosom—"

Adonis rolled his eyes. "Here we go."

The monster scowled, then cleared his throat. "Deep within my bosom, I hold feelings of affection. Yet other passions stir me like any other man—not least among them a venomous rage. Despair imbues my every thought, and I yearn for revenge. I shall draw sweet pleasure by indulging myself in your shrieks and torment as you die. For within my bosom—"

The rest of his monologue was cut off by a swing from Adonis's sword. The blade cut his meaty arm, slicing into it. The monster roared, even though no blood poured from his body.

"Stop it with the bosoms," Adonis snarled. "You sound like a twat."

The monster staggered back, but the blow hardly seemed to affect him. In the next moment, he was lunging for Adonis, wielding his torch like a weapon. "I shall incinerate you and relish the cries of your torment!"

I pulled an arrow from my quiver, nocking it. "I take it your death powers aren't working on him."

"No. He is unnatural, and so is his soul."

I loosed my arrow, and it found its mark in his chest. He kept stumbling onward, moving toward me with his torch, and I stepped backward.

"The gods should never have given the fire of knowledge to mankind," he bellowed. "For look what they've done with it. The world reviles me, and anguish pierces me to the marrow! I am malicious only because—"

Adonis swung for him again, his blade carving into the monster's side. "Please stop talking."

The monster howled, but he seemed undeterred. I nocked another arrow, and it sailed into his chest, protruding next to the other one. "I am alone!" he cried, thrusting his torch at us. "And palely loitering!"

The weapons weren't stopping him. Still, there was only one of him, and two of us.

At least, there *had* been only one of him. I gaped as more monsters stumbled from the shadows, their feet slamming against the stones.

"I thought you said you were tormented by solitude?" snapped Adonis. "There are dozens of you. What in the gods' names are you complaining about?"

"Each of us equally tormented by cruel solitude, for within our bosoms—"

One of my arrows slammed into his jaw, cutting off his rambling. But as soon as it did, I felt a searing heat scorching the back of my arm.

I whirled to find a new monster thrusting his torch at me. "The fires of knowledge burn you!"

"That is actual, literal fire," I shouted, gripping my arm. "You fucking knob-end."

Lucky for me, the rain had dampened my clothing, so nothing ignited.

But now, more monsters surrounded us, each one of them

waving a torch and banging on about their bosoms and cruel visages. Most importantly, they all looked eager to light us on fire. My heart raced, and I loosed arrow after arrow.

My arrows were flying uselessly into them, striking their hearts, their lungs. And it didn't make a godsdamned bit of difference, because they just kept lumbering on, waving their torches.

They'd encircled us, closing us in, determined to burn us to death.

I backed up to Adonis, my arrow still raised. "Now might be a good time to use those wings."

"Already? I thought we were doing well here."

"Do you really want to stand here listening to their monologues?"

"You have a point."

In the next moment, his arms were encircling me, and he lifted me into the air, wings beating the rainy air. As he lifted me above the castle, I stared down at the undead mob below us. We'd escaped them, but they blocked the only entrance I could see to the castle.

I had no idea what could kill these fuckers, until another bolt of lightning cracked the sky.

I had a feeling that electrical pulses had given life to these corpses. Was it possible that a powerful electrical current could also overwhelm them—overloading their synapses?

That electricity between the palace spires pulsed again, igniting the wires between the towers. As it did, an idea began to spark in my mind.

Rainwater covered the ground below us. Water conducted electricity, right?

The storm hammered against us, and I shifted in Adonis's arms. "Can you bring us over to those wires? The ones with the electricity running between them?"

"Why?" he murmured in my ear. "Are you planning on ending it all after listening to them speak for too long?"

"No, I think I have an idea." I reached behind my back, pulling an arrow from my quiver.

I'd just have to be *very* quick, or I really would end it all.

Adonis soared toward the wires that stretched between the spires. I watched them carefully, getting a feel for the rhythm of the electrical pulses. I had about five seconds between each one. "When I say 'now,' bring me right down to the wire."

"Are you going to tell me what in the gods' names this is about?"

"You'll just have to trust me."

When the next burst of electricity sparked and snapped along the wire, I said, "Now!"

One.

Adonis swooped lower until we were just over the copper wire.

Two.

I ripped it out of its mooring, the copper biting into my fingers.

Three. I quickly tied the wire to the end of my arrow.

Four. I raised my bow, then loosed the arrow. It soared into the crowd of monsters, touching down on the wet ground.

Five.

The next electrical pulse burst along the line, racing down the copper until it ignited within the crowd. Electricity singed the air as it surged through the monsters' bodies, and the scent of burning flesh curled all around us.

One by one, they fell to the ground.

"There." I nuzzled my face against Adonis's. "They're not tormented by solitude anymore."

"You could say that."

"Because they're dead," I added.

"I understood, yes."

During the next gap between electrical pulses, I yanked on the wire, pulling the arrow up from the ground. With one shot from my bow, it soared over the castle's spires in the other direction.

And just like that, I'd cleared the ground for our landing.

23

He lowered us to the ground, and we stood before the fallen pile of monsters.

Honestly, there was no better antidote to an aphrodisiac than a pile of scorched, undead and re-dead monsters. The stench and the charred remains managed to dampen any remaining lust that might have heated my body. At least, for now.

I glanced at Adonis's hand, grimacing when I saw the blood still flowing from his palm. If we spent too long here, would he actually become mortal? And what other disturbing creatures would we run into?

I stared at the castle entrance. Unlike a traditional castle with an iron gate or portcullis, this one had a wooden door inset into a stone opening. The stone doorframe had been carved to look like some sort of clown with sharp teeth. I shuddered. I was no psychological expert, but clown-fascination never seemed like the hallmark of mental stability or social adjustment.

An electric light flickered above us, and I eyed the buzzer. While I was mentally calculating another complex plan with my bow and arrow—in case something came running for us—Adonis reached over me, pushing the buzzer.

"Just like that. You're ringing the doorbell."

He shrugged.

After a few beats of silence, the castle door creaked open on its own, revealing an empty stone hallway. There were no defenses here to deter us. Had the king been expecting us? It only reinforced my sense that he'd been watching us.

We crossed into the hall, where the tall ceiling arched high above us. A crimson velvet carpet stretched out over the floor like the tongue of an enormous beast. I breathed in deeply, that floral aphrodisiac heating my blood again.

Lightbulbs crackled and sparked from the arched ceiling, and a rhythmic beat from distant music pulsed in the air. I glanced at the carpet, thinking of Adonis's tongue on my thighs. A smile curled my lips.

It was at this moment that I looked down at myself, realizing that at some point—probably in the last few seconds—I'd pulled down the top of my dress, exposing my sheer bra. The strap of my bow carved between my breasts. My nipples were standing at attention, and for a moment, the sight of them distracted me until I yanked my top up once more. *Keep it together, Agent Hudole.*

Adonis's hand around my waist didn't help the situation, and he leaned into me, breathing in deeply. I indulged myself in a quick kiss on his neck, licking his skin, tasting a hint of salt. Then, I forced myself to pull away again, thinking of the stench of scorched corpses.

Stay focused, Ruby. Stay focused. Corpse bosoms and scorched flesh.

At the top of the stairs, the doors opened into a red-velvet-draped hall. It had the shabby, faded grandeur of an old music hall—in fact, maybe it *was* an old music hall, crammed with people in vibrant clothing. Voices echoed off the high ceiling. A stage stood at one end of the hall, and balconies and box seats hung above us. Faded green and red paint chipped off the wood. I *liked* it here. In fact, I didn't really want to leave.

"This place is amazing," I breathed.

I could almost envision myself on the stage, giving the burlesque performance of my life. Some black tassels, a fan dance. In fact, I had the strongest urge to get up there right now.

Adonis's eyes were on me, blazing with intensity, and I could feel his magic strengthen, licking over my body. "It's going to be hard to focus in here," he said.

I licked my lips. "You have a knack for understatements."

Chandeliers with sparking lightbulbs illuminated the crowd. All around us, women wore thigh-high stockings and short, bright frocks. They sipped from bright green drinks, their cheeks and lips painted red. The men wore suits, many of them with thin mustaches and slick hair.

In corners and under tables all around the room, men and women were groping and straddling each other.

Waitresses tottered around the room—their movements jerky, just like the women I'd seen outside. The waitresses' skin looked stretched over their bones, nearly translucent. They were the undead ones—corpses raised from the dead by the necromancer.

Unlike the waitresses, all the guests were alive. I stared at a woman climbing onto a tabletop and beckoning a man closer, her eyes half-lidded with lust.

I licked my lips, my body growing warm, swelling against my sodden dress. In here, the perfumed scent overwhelmed me, and my breath quickened.

A haze of sweet-smelling smoke filled the air. Why were we here, again? That's right, we were here to enjoy ourselves.

A waitress lurched past us, and I plucked a glowing green

drink from the tray. I took a sip, savoring the hint of anise, before Adonis snatched it from my hand. "Bad idea, Ruby."

His sharp gray eyes brought me down to earth again.

"Right." I blinked a few times, surveying the crowd. Although the guests were alive, everyone's eyes held a glazed expression.

Adonis leaned down, whispering in my ear. "The longer we stay here, the harder it will be to leave."

"I was starting to get that impression." Whoever ruled this place seemed like he was into both necromancy and mind control. And ... orgies. "Any idea where we are yet?"

Adonis furrowed his brow. "I'm beginning to get a sense. I think we may have wandered into the realm of a phantom king named Spring-Heeled Jack."

"Who?"

"In the nineteenth century, women all over London reported being attacked by a winged creature who'd fly at them and grope their breasts." Adonis linked his arm through mine, and we started walking. He leaned in, whispering in my ear as we moved deeper into the hall. "Sometimes he breathed out fire, blue and white flames. After a bit of grop-ing, he'd bound away again. The rumors were that he was a hedonist who lived in almost total isolation. So, he built himself a small kingdom of revived corpses to keep him company and to indulge with him, only occasionally venturing out into London to claw at women's breasts."

Gods. "Oh, he sounds lovely. I hope we get to meet him."

"Now," added Adonis, "it seems he's found himself some living playthings from among the desperate resistance. And they're completely under his thrall."

In all likelihood, the drinks played a role in the mind control.... In fact, I was having a harder time than ever thinking clearly. Warmth flooded my veins.

Adonis was talking to me, but I couldn't focus on the

content of what he was saying, just the rich timbre of his voice. It rumbled over my skin, caressing me. My back arched as I walked, hips swaying to the pulsing music.

Cool air whispered over my skin, and I realized I'd pulled up the hem of my dress. If I hadn't been wearing the bow slung over my back, I'd have pulled it off completely.

Now, Adonis's eyes looked as glazed as mine, and he stared at my body, fingers skimming my waist. Forget acting like angels. We were animals, and we might as well give into it.

I started to tug up the hem of his shirt, but he grabbed my wrists, leaning in to me, whispering in my ear.

Something about *resist ... resist*....

Right. The resistance. That's why we were here.

How could I clear this fucking fog from my mind? Adonis used physical pain, Kratos used mental pain. Right?

I closed my eyes, summoning my worst memories. The day Marcus had died. The fear in my mother's eyes when I'd bitten her arm. Adonis lying dead after I'd killed him.

Pain tightened my chest, and my mind began to clear again. I breathed deeply, tears stinging my eyes.

I smoothed out my dress. "Okay. I'm with you now. What were you saying to me?"

"You met some of the members of the resistance. Do you see them here?"

"Give me a sec." I grabbed Adonis by the hand, moving around in the crowd, until a spark of recognition ignited in my mind.

There, sipping from a glass of bright green cocktail, I found one of the leaders of the resistance. She now wore a lacy black dress, and her dark brown eyes held a glazed expression.

Bingo. At least I knew now we were in the right place, which meant all the reanimated corpses had been worth it.

"Lila!" I grabbed her arm, trying to catch her attention, but she just licked her lips.

The keen intelligence I'd seen in her expression before had disappeared. She sipped her cocktail, blinking at Adonis. "Yeah, so, like ... I think I spilled something on my tits, but I don't really care. Has that ever happened to you?"

Adonis's magic thickened in the air. "No, as a matter of fact. But we need to get you out of here. You and the rest of the resistance."

I reached for her cocktail glass. "You need to stop drinking this."

Lila scrunched her nose. "I don't know, because, like ... it makes me feel good. I don't really want to have to think, and this makes me not have to think. I kind of feel like I want a jam sandwich, but it might make my hands sticky." She began swaying rhythmically to the music again.

I caught a glimpse of Brianna, who spun in a circle, sloshing her green cocktail over the dance floor. "I think I'm flying!"

And this was what was left of our army.

❦ 24 ❦

I frowned at Adonis. "So, I think the entire resistance is here, shitfaced and boning each other under tables. Any ideas? Because my instinct is just to start slapping them all until they snap out of it."

"It's not the worst idea you've ever had."

"It's not, is it?" I bit my lip. "Pain can throw people out of ecstatic states. You know all about that."

"Do you want me to stab them all in the heart? Because I think we might find our army at a disadvantage once they've all expired."

I shook my head. "We can use mental pain. Just like Kratos does. What if I showed them visions that would shock them out of it? I can use my illusion powers, now, and show them exactly what will happen to them if they don't get back to England and start fighting back."

Adonis looked down at his bleeding palm. "Try it. We don't have many other options, and we're running out of time."

I summoned my glamour—the one where I could project illusions—and conjured up images of what the future would hold if Metatron were allowed to carry out his plan.

On the stage, in front of the red curtain, I created an image of London, and one of Westminster Cathedral's walls now stood before us on the stage. I littered the streets with bodies—piles of them, rotting before the Cathedral. I scanned the crowd around me, finding that they seemed completely unimpressed by the image. They pretty much kept swaying on the dance floor, tonguing each other.

"Wrong tactic," I said to Adonis. "The dead are too faceless, and no one cares about faceless dead people. I need to show them the deaths of people they care about."

I'd start with Lila first. She was both their leader, and absolutely adorable. I had no doubt that many of the people she led cared about her—particularly some of the men, given the way they were following her around right now.

I flicked my fingers, bringing up a new image—this one of Lila standing in a road. Aereus appeared on his red horse, galloping over the pavement. He drew his sword, and it burst into flames. Lila drew a gun, shooting at him, but the bullets didn't stop him.

Aereus carved his blade through her neck, and her body fell to the earth.

A few screams echoed off the tall ceiling. Good, good. I was starting to get to them.

Adonis stroked his chin. "His sword doesn't burn like that."

"I was taking artistic license."

"You made him cooler than he is."

"Shhh ... I'm concentrating."

Now, I summoned an image of Brianna and Amber, running from Metatron. He raised his hands in the air, eyes blazing with flames, and he lit the two women on fire. They fell to the ground, their bodies writhing with fiery torment.

More screams erupted over the hall.

Adonis cocked his head. "The fiery eyes were a nice touch. Also inaccurate."

For my *pièce de resistance*, I plucked random members from the crowd, and envisioned them in the worst possible scenarios. Aereus breaking them on his torture wheel, pulling their bodies apart on the rack. Bodies being trampled, hanged, death in the streets. I conjured up the most disturbing images I could and displayed them over the hall. I nearly made myself sick with creative ways to maim and mutilate.

Screams erupted all over the hall, cutting through the miasma of euphoria.

When I'd finished, Adonis was staring at me with a mixture of horror and admiration. "I'm not sure if I want to kiss you or run away from you right now."

One by one, each person in the crowd began snapping out of their trances. Their eyes became alert, and suddenly they were pulling up their pants and smoothing out their dresses, making mortified eye contact with the people around them. Nervous chatter broke out, and a sense of pure panic tinged the air. I let the images continue to play on the stage so they wouldn't slip back into euphoria, keeping them focused on the real danger that lay ahead of them.

"Now, someone needs to tell them what's going on," said Adonis. "But I don't think it should come from me."

I reached out, grabbing Lila's arm. If they were going to listen to anyone right now, it would be one of their leaders.

She stared at me, her eyes wide, body trembling. "How did I end up here?"

"You've been mind-controlled by a phantom king and everyone has been fucking in a music hall. Easy mistake; it could happen to anyone."

Her jaw dropped. "*What?*"

"Look, you jumped into a sketchy realm, here. And the

truth is, we don't have a lot of time left. Metatron is going to destroy the rest of the earth in just a few days, and we need to fight back. Now." I pointed at the stage. "Or everything you saw up there will come true."

"Not the flaming sword," added Adonis. "But the rest of it."

Lila bit her lip. "How do I know I can trust you?"

"Look at this situation." I waved at the crowd. "It's not a good one. And I'm the one getting you out of here."

Around us, the members of the resistance were panicking.

Lila grabbed my arm. "I'll have to find our mages to get us out of here. If we can find the portal—"

"I'll get us out of here faster," Adonis interrupted. "We just need you to tell your people what's going on so they'll follow."

"Right." Lila glanced at the balconies above us. "Some of my memories are starting to come back, now. There's a man with claw-like fingers, flames shooting out of his mouth. He swoops in and ... I can't quite remember." Her body had gone rigid with tension. "We need to get out of here before *he* comes. I can't quite remember who he is, or what he does, but—"

"Spring-Heeled Jack," Adonis cut in. "Necromancer phantom-king pervert with claws. Now we're up to speed. I'm going outside to create a portal just on the other side of the undead, re-dead corpse pile. Lead everyone out there as soon as you can." And with that, Adonis took off, slipping through the crowd.

Lila began clambering to the top of a table, then cupped her hands around her mouth. "Members of the resistance!" Her voice echoed off the hall.

The panicked murmurs in the hall began to simmer down.

"We've made a terrible mistake," Lila shouted. "We never should have come here. We need to get back to London, now.

We may only have a few days left before—" She pointed at the stage. "Before all that shite happens for real. One of our allies is creating a portal for us right now, just outside—"

A shriek cut through the air, and all heads turned to the ceiling. A blur of black and white swooped above us, zooming between the chandeliers.

Spring-Heeled Jack, I presumed.

That's when all hell broke loose.

An undead waitress next to me dropped her tray, and glass smashed on the floor. Her expression grew furious, and she pulled a knife from her garter belt.

Oh, balls. The phantom king was turning his undead servants on us.

From the darkest corners of the music hall, towering monsters—like the ones we'd seen outside—tottered into the crowd. I stared as one of them picked up a bespectacled member of the resistance, bashing him against the wall.

Some of the monsters brandished torches at the crowd members, bellowing about their tormented souls.

The monsters were turning on us.

"Out! Now!" I shrieked at the resistance. But no one could hear me above the din.

"My life is an accumulation of anguish!" One of the monsters boomed. "Since I cannot be loved, I will be feared!"

Oh, for fuck's sake.

"Start leading them outside," I shouted to Lila. She followed my command, already elbowing her way to the hall exit.

My pulse raced. Pandemonium had erupted, and I considered readying an arrow. But in close quarters like this, it wasn't the best weapon.

Unless.... If all the monsters and undead waitresses were following the phantom king's command, maybe I could just take him out. Would they all simply collapse?

I pulled an arrow from my quiver, then whirled to find the nearest torch-wielding monster. I lit the tip of the arrow in his flames, then nocked it. I scanned the ceiling, watching the phantom zoom between the chandeliers. He moved so quickly I could hardly track him, but I locked my gaze on him as he leapt down into the crowd. He wore a black cape and pointed velvet cap, and his eyes flashed with flames.

He plunged to the ground, grabbing for a woman's breasts with his clawed hands. She tried to land a punch, but he leapt toward the ceiling again before she could make contact.

Weird prick.

With my gaze trained on him, I loosed the flaming arrow. It grazed his cape, igniting. He shrieked, his eyes blazing, then set his sights on me.

I nocked another arrow, but he was already zooming toward me. With his cape flaming, he flew faster—too fast for me to track. He slammed into me and knocked me into the ground. The speed of his flight had already extinguished the flames.

I tried to shove him off me, but he slammed a fist into my skull. My thoughts went a bit woozy.

Quick as a flash, his clawed fingers were around my throat. He started to spit fire, but I kneed him hard in the balls.

He howled, and tears sprang from his eyes. As I looked into his face, my mind began to fog once more, clouded with a vision of a euphoric cabaret, women dancing in short skirts.

"Why did you have to ruin this for me?" Spittle flew from his mouth. "I lived here alone for far too long. The corpses were my friends." His lip curled, a faraway look in his eyes. "When the Great Nightmare began, I had so many corpses to choose from. All these beautiful dead women, here to serve my needs. Their flesh ready for the groping, no arguments from them." He clawed at my breasts. "But then I thought, why limit myself to the dead, when I could use my scientific knowledge to control the living? A whole army here to keep me company...."

I gritted my teeth, trying to focus. I needed to shove the cabaret visions out of my mind. *Blood on the pavement. Adonis's dead body*....

With images of death in my mind clearing my thoughts, I brought my knee up into his balls once more. The phantom's eyes widened, and I slammed my fist hard into his face. Then, I tugged on his cape, pulling him off me. Lightning-fast, I leapt up. I snatched an arrow from my quiver, then fired it into his chest.

As I stood over him, his body simply disappeared, leaving behind only a wisp of smoke. The floral scent intensified in the air.

When I looked around me, I found the crowd streaming out of the hall, fighting back against the monsters. I ran with them, struggling to keep my thoughts focused.

At last, we burst free into the open air. Rain hammered down and lightning cracked the sky. Adonis had created a portal—an enormous, black whirlpool. One by one, the humans plunged into it, not knowing exactly where they were going, or if we could be trusted, but only that they had to get the fuck away from the torch-wielding monsters.

Just after the last of the humans plunged into the portal, I grabbed Adonis's hand and jumped in with him.

❧ 25 ❧

W e climbed out of the freezing river, dripping
with sludgy water. By the time Adonis and I got
out, Lila was already mid-speech, the entire
resistance milling around the river's edge. Lila stood on a tree
stump, shouting through her cupped hands.

It didn't seem like she was getting through to anyone,
considering the entire crowd was jabbering over her. She
needed help.

I crossed to her. "Lila."

She turned to me, fear shining in her eyes. "They don't
understand what's happening. And I'm not sure I do, either.
Can you explain it to them?"

I stepped onto the tree stump. "Members of the resistance!" I shouted, waiting for the crowd to fall into a reverent
hush.

That did not happen.

"Shut the fuck up, everyone!" I shouted.

And that also did not work. I stared out at the crowd of
resistance members, their colorful frocks soaked with river
water, makeup streaking the women's faces. Just like Lila, I

had no control over the panicked crowd. Maybe another visual would get their attention.

I took a deep breath, channeling my glamour magic. It tingled over my body as I summoned an image of a field of corpses—some of them with recognizable faces from the crowd before me. Aereus appeared from nowhere, his golden wings swooping behind him, flaming sword raised.

After he trampled the corpses, I envisioned them blackening and decomposing into the earth.

I could feel the mood dampen around me, turning from panic into complete despair. I swallowed hard. Perhaps I was hitting the mortality note a bit too hard. I had to lighten the mood with a bit of hope.

From the rotting corpse pile, I summoned the image of a golden flower—then another, and another. A field of golden flowers grew—then buildings, houses, a thriving city.

Life grows from death.

Now, a reverent hush *had* actually fallen over the crowd.

I cleared my throat. "I've been showing you images of what might happen in the next few days if we don't band together. I think you get the point now, right? We'll all die, probably in painful ways. But if we fight back—using whatever means necessary—we can survive this. And we can rebuild again. You may have to change and adapt—you might have to become something you're not. But we'll only win if we use every tool in our arsenal. Including adaptation. I'll let your leaders explain the rest to you, because—frankly, you don't even know who I am."

I nodded, stepping down from the tree stump, and gripped Lila by the shoulders. "Convince them. Convince them to become demons."

Okay, the speech had ended on kind of a lame note, but I think I had gotten the point across. For now, I was leaving out the part about how Kratos—the Hunter—would be leading them. The fact was, the Horseman of Conquest was a natural combat leader. He could survey the fighting from above, issue commands in their minds, coordinate it all with precision.

Just a bit inconvenient that he'd spent over a year trying to slaughter all of them with his dogs.

I moved deeper into the forest, searching for Adonis. It took me a moment to find him standing in the shadows of a towering oak, separated from the rest of the group. He was staring at something, but I couldn't quite see what.

Shivering, I crossed to him and stood by his side. He seemed to be staring into the dark forest.

"Umm ... is there something I'm missing here?" I asked.

"Don't you see it?" He reached out, stroking his fingertip against the air. As he did, a faint silvery ripple spread outward from his fingertips.

"What the hell is that?" I asked.

"A shield. I just have no idea who created it."

Well, this was interesting.

From the other side, an arrow slammed against the shield, and a crack began to form, splintering the air before us.

I stared down at the arrow on the other side of the shield. When I crouched down to inspect further, I could see that the shaft was carved with tiny Angelic markings.

Somewhere out there in the forest, the Heavenly Host wanted to shoot their way through this shield.

I turned, rushing back to Lila. She was milling around with people in the crowd, and I grabbed her by the arm. "What did they say?" I asked.

Her eyes were wide. "I think your disturbing displays of death might have actually worked. You scared the shit out of them."

WE CROSSED THE HALL TOWARD THE CELESTIAL ROOM, AND I could feel the tension rippling off Adonis.

As soon as we'd stepped inside the castle, Hazel had been there to excitedly give us the answer to our shield mystery. Apparently, Kratos had returned with our new potential allies. Rosalind and Caine had arrived while we'd been off fighting undead monsters. Rosalind had thrown up a shield to protect us from the Heavenly Host, and now Caine was waiting to meet with us for some sort of discussion.

In the stone hallway, Adonis had gone completely silent.

"You don't seem particularly thrilled about seeing Caine," I said.

"He hates angels. He used to seduce them just to make them fall. Muriel was among them."

I frowned. "Has it occurred to you that maybe Muriel would be better as a demon? Because she kind of sucks as an angel."

"Really?" His eyebrows shot up. "She's not that bad."

"She's awful. But anyway, we need Caine to help us, so maybe you should let go of whatever happened five hundred years ago. Time to move on."

"I've moved on. I'm just not a hundred percent sure we can trust these people. You don't know what he's like."

I frowned. "Marcus trusted him. He must have changed after a few centuries. It's a long time to most people, you know."

The doors to the Celestial Room swung open. From the glass dome, moonlight streamed into the center of the room, piercing the incubus's dark aura that wafted around him like smoke.

Caine sat with his feet on the table, a glass of whiskey in his hand. Dark curls framed his chiseled features. He had similar coloring to Adonis—but his eyes were an eerie silver and his body was narrower, lips a little fuller. Shadowy magic bloomed around him, darkening the air. In his presence, the air felt a little cooler, and I shivered, hugging myself. For a moment, the ghost of dark wings appeared behind him. His magic smelled like a lightning storm.

Instantly—at the sight of Adonis—he narrowed his strange, pale eyes, and rose from his chair. They walked toward each other.

The two men squared off toward each other, in some kind of gorgeous alpha male stare-off.

"Incubus," said Adonis. "I believe we've met before."

"Horseman," said Caine, managing to lace the word with a considerable amount of disgust. "What do I know you from? Oh, that's right. You tried to kill me. Didn't work. I guess killing a demigod was a little harder than you thought, wasn't it?"

Well. This was going well.

Adonis slid his hands into his pockets, looking perfectly at ease, even though I could feel the tension rippling off his body. "Right. How could I forget? Little Caine, born in a whorehouse, descended from the god of the void. What a charming combination."

"You could write my biography. Is it just me, or are you fascinated by me?" Caine lifted his glass. "I'm drinking your whiskey. Am I right in thinking your kind isn't supposed to indulge? You wouldn't want to risk turning into a scary demon like me, would you? You might find yourself the star of stories meant to scare children, or perhaps enjoying yourself. How horrifying."

Adonis sauntered forward another step, his gait easy. "Remind me. How long has it been since you served as the Queen of Maremount's whore?"

"Just a few centuries. It was right before I tossed her body out the tower window." He sipped his whiskey. "Ah, now I remember why I love angels so much. Being judged by you is so much fun. Let's not indulge or enjoy life. The angels might frown at us." Caine stepped closer, his silver eyes trained on Adonis. "You'd never truly give in to pleasure or passion, now, would you? Always holding back. Does your girlfriend mind your restraint?"

Adonis's smile faltered a little. "Angels have a sense of responsibility that a waste of life like you would never understand."

Caine quirked a smile. "Is that the same sense of responsibility you feel when killing scores of people with plagues?"

I clapped my hands together. "Okay, so, we're all a little cranky today. A few naps and some cookies would be in order. But we're all supposed to be on the same side, aren't we?"

Shadows whirled around Caine. "You're not cursed anymore, horseman, are you? I can't see the curse on you."

"I pulled the curses off Adonis and Kratos," I said. "They're both free now."

Caine cocked his head. "You've found a way to fuck with impunity. Maybe I like your priorities."

"You haven't changed much, have you?" said Adonis. "Your mother must be so proud."

Caine shrugged. "She was a literal whore, so who knows. And yes, I have changed. I command the Lilinor army now, and I'm married to a woman whose powers exceed my own. Which is why we're here."

I crossed my arms. "So, if you don't want to work with angels, why are you here?"

"My wife, Rosalind, is fond of humans. I have no idea why. She wanted to find out what you have to say in case she can help protect them." Caine looked at me for the first time, and his pale eyes bored into me. "An angel who loves a fae. Now that is interesting. Life and death, pleasure and restraint. Maybe death-horse here is more interesting than I'd given him credit for."

I took a deep breath. "Okay. Well, that's all the pleasantries out of the way; now let's get down to the real issue. Rosalind's shield is protecting us, but the angels' arrows are already cracking its surface."

"I don't see how that's possible." A female voice turned my head. I looked around to see a beautiful brunette woman. The faintest hints of colored magic whirled off her athletic body in fine tendrils—just wisps and glimmers. Somehow, she exuded power and vulnerability at the same time. "The shield shouldn't be able to crack. Caine and I built it together. We've been protecting Lilinor with a shield for years, and we're pretty good at it by now." She crossed to her husband, putting her arm around his waist.

"But you've never encountered an enemy like Metatron," said Adonis. "His angelic magic can destroy anything. He creates chaos, breaks things down. He will make you feel insane and destroy the fabric of the world around him."

"And we've got about two days until he wrecks the entire world." I shivered in my freezing gown. "Metatron is going to try to kill us all, and then slaughter everyone else on earth. In a couple of days, he'll be going on a killing spree all over the earth. Starting with London. We need your help to stop that from happening."

Caine sipped his whiskey. "Why not just escape to one of the magical realms? We were safe in Lilinor."

Adonis shook his head. "We'd never get every living creature on earth into a magical realm. And in any case, Metatron will probably come after those, too. He can move in and out of realms at will, and he's hell-bent on destroying demons. Lilinor is not safe, even with your shield up."

I could see Caine visibly stiffen. He wanted to protect his home. Good. He'd fight harder that way.

I crossed my arms. "Look, outside this castle, we have an entire army of humans who are reluctantly willing to transform into demons because they're terrified of dying. They're willing to fight with us."

Rosalind stared at me. "And you think they can defeat the Heavenly Host?"

"Not quite," I said. "But I think we can stop their death march for now."

"They're immortal." Adonis met my gaze. "Only Ruby can defeat the Heavenly Host. She just needs a little more time to work on it."

At least, I hoped to the seven hells that time was all I needed.

🍃 2 6 🍃

Kratos stood above me, his copper wings swooping behind him.

I sat in the grass, looking up at him. When speaking to Conquest, staring up from the ground only seemed like the natural order of things.

His body glowed with ethereal copper. "Have you convinced the members of the resistance to let themselves become transformed into immortal beings?"

"I showed them some images of their deaths."

"I saw. You do realize Aereus's sword can't really shoot flames?"

"What is it with you horsemen and realism? I took some liberties. It gets the point across. Anyway, it worked to set the stage. Lila, one of their leaders, did the rest of the convincing."

He cocked his head. "You know, I never before would have imagined that mortal beasts would take such convincing. Who *wouldn't* want to become a superior creature?"

"Right. Particularly when you all have such charming personalities," I said. "But, yes, they're on board now.

Rosalind is already transforming them, one by one." I glanced at the fracturing shield once more. "It's, unfortunately, kind of a long process, and that thing won't last long."

"And they know that I'm to be their leader, right?"

I shook my head. "Not yet. I'm thinking that the news that the Hunter is their new leader will be a last-minute revelation. When they're too committed to back out."

"Devious. I like it." He frowned. "It hasn't escaped my attention that you tend to leave out crucial bits of information quite a lot. You tend to just tell one part of the story."

"The stories we tell shape reality. We have to be careful with them. So let's make sure this ends up being a story about victory, shall we?" I glanced at my legs. A silver chain attached cuffs on my ankle to a silver loop in the ground. In case I tried to rip the chains right out of the earth, I'd asked him to add a few spikes inside the loose cuff. The pain could rip me out of any kind of feral trance—one that might lead to my death.

Of course, I'd left out the "I might die" part of the story.

"You're sure these things will hold?" I asked.

"I've protected them with angelic magic. Only an angel would be able to get you out of them."

"You'd better fly away from me, now. And make sure Adonis is nowhere near me. If I explode with light, the Old Gods might kill you."

"Good luck." Kratos beat his wings, then took off into the sky. I watched him fly away, his copper glow growing smaller as he swooped over the castle's turrets.

I took a deep breath, staring up at the fracturing shield. I didn't want to practice this magic, but I had to. Once Metatron broke through, he and Aereus would come for us. First, they'd capture me. They'd torture me until I broke mentally, then they'd try to force me to kill Adonis and Kratos with my powers. Would I do it, if pushed hard enough? I really didn't want to find out, but I suspected everyone had a breaking point.

Then, they'd kill me and Hazel. In other words, a quick death was better than this outcome. When I thought of what could go wrong, panic rose in my chest.

My heart raced out of control. I tried to shut out my frantic thoughts, to center myself by tuning into the world around me. If I couldn't calm myself, I wouldn't be of any use to anyone. Right now, I had a task to achieve, and I needed to be able to focus on something other than my own probable death.

Focus on the moment. I lay in the grass, staring up at the night sky. Buttercups dotted the grasses nearby.

The stars looked a little different tonight, with the faint silver sheen of the shield. It also seemed like my vision was becoming increasingly keen ever since I'd gotten the gemstones. Another deep, centering breath. Now, I could see it all—particularly vivid was the bright swath of the Milky Way.

I exhaled, trying to force out my feelings of panic.

At least, until another angel soared above the shield, shooting an arrow at the dome of magic, just above my head. Particles of the shield fragmented, raining down on me.

Caine and Rosalind might be gods or demigods or whatever, but their shitty shield needed a little help from the Old Gods. And now, it was time to try to summon it.

I closed my eyes, channeling the magic of the Old Gods. Faintly, the gemstones in my forehead began heating. The song of the Old Gods whispered in the back of my mind.

Then, it fizzled out again. I blew a strand of hair out of my eyes. Seemed like I was bouncing between not being able to summon the magic at all and letting it overwhelm me until it was going to rip my mind and body apart.

Maybe I'd gone a little too far with calming myself down.

The other times I'd summoned the Old Gods' power, I'd been blazing with adrenaline, scared for either myself or Adonis.

Just like with the resistance, fear could be a powerful motivator.

I sat up in the grass. Instead of channeling the Old Gods' light, I summoned an illusion—something that would make me wild with fury and fear. Adonis, on his knees, as Aereus slammed his sword through his head—just like I'd seen in Paris.

Already, my canines were growing longer, my feral side taking over.

At the sight of blood and gore before me, a mixture of rage and panic began to roil in my veins, and the gemstones grew hotter. My blood roared in my ears, and wild power ripped through me.

Images of a garden paradise bloomed in my mind like wildflowers, and I ran along the river's edge, hunting an angel....

I snarled, light beaming from my body. The symphony of the Old Gods built and crested in my mind. And as it did, cracks formed in my body, and I could feel that the light was going to destroy me from the inside out.

Creatures like me were never meant to toy with divine magic like this. The Old Gods wanted to punish me for stealing their magic.

As I felt the magic tearing me apart, it brought out the beast in me, desperate to live. I wanted to tear through flesh, I wanted—

A sharp pain in my ankle snapped me out of it. Jolted out of my trance, I stared down at the blood pouring from my ankle, staining the yellow buttercup petals.

So. That had gone well.

Frustration tightened my chest. *Well, this is fucking pointless.*

I was a Bringer of Light, unable to use my powers without sacrificing my life.

The delicious smell of myrrh began to soothe me, and without turning my head, I knew Adonis was there.

"Still working on it, are you?" The moonlight sparked in his gray eyes.

"I told you to stay away from me while I was practicing. I'm not quite there yet. But I think I'm making progress." I heaved a heavy breath. "I'm lying. I'm making no progress whatsoever. Do you really think we can defeat Metatron? The resistance isn't even trained soldiers. They're just ordinary people who've been starving in hovels for years, eating rats."

Adonis stared up at the sky. "The truth is, I don't know what will happen, Ruby. But if you'd asked me months ago if I thought it would ever be possible to remove my curse and fall in love with a fae, I would've said no."

"The Old Gods are powerful," I said, "but I wasn't born to wield that power. Maybe humans and fae like me were never meant to have the tools of the divine beings. Maybe our minds can't handle it."

"I thought you didn't believe in destinies like that? Anyway, maybe there's power in opposite forces joining together. Look at us. You and I are the beginning and the end, we are life and death. We are strangely perfect together." He leaned down, ripping the silver chains from the earth. Then, he swept me into his arms, and I breathed in his delicious scent. His warmth and powerful magic enveloped me.

I slid down his body, then lay back on the grass. I held out my hand to Adonis. He lay next to me, his body warming mine. I curled into him, resting my head on his shoulder, and put my hand over his heart to feel its beat. Then, I turned my head to stare up at the stars blazing above us. I focused on the Milky Way, picturing it as it would appear from outer space, elegant swoops curving around a gaping black hole at the center.

Once again, I saw the seeds of death in the world around me. "Someday, everything in the universe will fall into a black hole, ripped apart by gravity. All the fires in the stars will die out, and the universe will lie a cold, abandoned wasteland. In the end, chaos consumes us all."

"You're in a cheerful mood, aren't you?"

A bright star above us flickered like a Christmas tree light. I pointed to it. "Do you see that? It's about to die. We're witnessing the death of a star."

"You're witnessing the death of a star two thousand years ago," he pointed out. "It died when I was still young. You're seeing its echo. And there are stars born out there that we can't yet see. Their creation is like us—a balance of forces, fusion and gravity."

He turned on his side, and his hand found its way to my waist.

"First you romanticize nature, now it's all death. If you can find a balance, maybe you can control your powers better. Nature isn't life or death. It's both. Accept your feral side. Accept your monstrous side. Neither of us are perfect. We are distinctly imperfect. You and I are both destructive, but that's not all we are. That's not the limit."

He traced his fingertips over my waist, and my blood heated.

❧ 2 7 ❧

"When I first saw you in the streets of London," said Adonis, "I saw your savage side. You were covered in blood, disguised as a demon. But there was life there, too—a spark of the divine in your eyes. You enthralled me. You woke something in my mind that I'd tried to keep dormant. You were dangerous to me. And even so, I took such a pleasure in killing the redcaps who wanted to hurt you. I will always take pleasure in killing anyone who wants to hurt you."

I quirked a smile. "Same. I'd quite happily eat Aereus's face off."

Adonis's eyebrows shot up. "I'd do it a bit more elegantly than you would, of course. And yet, even with your feral nature, you have an elegant side, too. When you danced for me, I couldn't take my eyes off the beauty of your body and the way it moved, the divine inspiration beneath every twirl. The way the fabric moved over your delicate skin, the light shining from behind the darkness in your eyes." He brushed his fingertips over my body, over my chest. "The flush of your chest. I knew there was a mystery there, one I needed to explore. You made me feel alive again, and vulnerable again. And then you pulled me back from the underworld. You had the power and the courage to raise Death from the dead. If anyone can take on Metatron, it's you."

"So you don't think we're bad for each other anymore? That we make each other too vulnerable?"

"When I smelled your blood all over the stones in Paris, I hadn't felt that sort of terror since my mother died. It swallowed me whole. I felt my heart breaking. The beauty that had awoken me again, that had revived me—it was just gone. So, yes, love is a vulnerability, but it's also my reason for living. And, yes, everything will end someday. In the end, even the immortals will be ripped apart by chaos. But we're here now—sparks of light in the darkness." He pointed at the stars. "And while we're here, still alive, there is divine order all around us."

I stared up at the Milky Way, thinking of its perfect whorls. It was a sort of divine order out there, wasn't it? And maybe it was an answer to the chaos. Like Adonis had said, maybe perfection could be found in the balance of opposites: life and death, chaos and order.

I remembered reading something in a magazine long ago about Fibonacci numbers—a series in which each number was the sum of the two numbers that came before it. One, one, two, three, five, eight, and so on. And when you divided them together, you got the golden ratio. Nature had a habit of using the golden ratio to create beautiful, elegant patterns of a predictable order. The swoops of seashells, the curves of floral patterns—natural beauty mimicked by painters.

I turned to my side, plucking a buttercup from the ground. There it was again, the spiraling, winding perfection of the petals.

Metatron created chaos wherever he went. But there was order within the swirling patterns of the stars. This math was the voice of the gods—celestial and earthly gods alike. If you knew where to look, you could find divinity in nature.

I twirled the buttercup in front of my eyes. I had power over plants, didn't I? Maybe nature could combat the chaos after all.

An idea began germinating my mind. "I want to try something."

"Oh?"

"I want to see exactly what I can do with plants. Buttercups, wild grasses, vines."

"I love you, Ruby, but I'm not sure we're going to defeat Metatron's immortal army with plants."

I frowned. "A minute ago, you were expressing complete confidence in me. What happened to that?"

"Well, you started talking about buttercups."

I sat up straight. "Maybe they're the answer to the chaos. There is order here. Have you heard of the Fibonacci sequence? Every number is the sum of the two numbers that came before it, and that gives us the golden ratio. It's in the distance between the whorls of stars in the Milky Way, or the spirals in a seashell. You can see it in the patterns of plants. Think about the number of petals that show up on a flower—it's usually one of those numbers. Whoever created the material world that we see around us used this pattern, over and over again. I think this is our answer."

He ran his fingertips up my arm, from my elbow up to my wrist, leaving trails of hot tingles in his wake. "And how do you plan to use these patterns?"

I shook my head. "I don't know yet. But I know I can control plants. I did it in your garden in Scotland, and when I killed Johnny." I took the buttercup and slowly stroked it down his perfect cheekbone.

It seemed to ignite something in him, and the next thing I

knew, lust shone in his eyes. He hissed a breath, giving me a look that said "I'm about to jump your bones."

Maybe practicing magic could be fun instead of just painful. In fact, I had the strongest urge now to watch my plants climbing all over his perfect body.

I waved my fingertips over the buttercups, and my skin tingled and sizzled with ancient magic. One of the buttercup stems began lengthening and snaking over Adonis's torso. Heat blazed in his eyes, and he ran a hand over his mouth, as if he was still restraining himself, still keeping himself leashed.

Part of me wanted to see if I could get him to fully let go. Maybe in order to coax him to unleash himself, I had to confine him myself. I'd be his restraints, until he fought against them with all his power.

I hooked my leg over his waist and climbed on top of him, my dress riding up nearly to my hips. From where he lay, he had a view of my lacy panties. Then, I unbuttoned his shirt and pulled it off, feeling the sensuous thrill of his magic caressing my body.

I tried to focus on my magic, even with the heat sizzling over my skin and his body between my thighs. "Watch this." I flicked my fingertips again, and buttercup stems surged from the ground, wrapping themselves around his wrists. I clenched my thighs around his abs, his skin warm against mine.

He let out a low snarl. "Are we done talking about buttercups?"

"No, we're just getting started. I'm going to teach you to listen to me when I talk about plants. I need to practice."

A wry smile curled his lips. "You do realize I have enough physical strength to break through buttercup stems.
"

I clenched my thighs tighter, then ran my hands up his

chest to his throat. "Don't disobey me. I killed a man with these thighs. Don't think I won't squeeze you to death."

"If I may put in a request for my method of execution," he said, his velvety voice stroking my body, "I'd like to die in the same way."

I cocked my head. "Noted. If I ever have to put you down, you can die between my thighs. And if you don't drop the cocky attitude, that might be sooner than you'd like."

"What attitude?"

"You're magic-shaming me. You have no faith in my plants. You're a plantist, in fact."

"When it comes to killing angels, I just don't think flowers are likely to be as effective as the magic that can literally hurl angels off the earth. Maybe that's a personal quirk of mine."

Sure. As long as you're fine with your girlfriend dying.

I narrowed my eyes. "You think you can break free from the buttercup stems? Try it."

Adonis's cocky smile still curled his lips—until he tried tugging on the stems. Then, the amusement left his features pretty fast.

Still straddling him, I straightened. "Like I said, you need to listen to me when I talk about plants."

"You can talk all you want. But I need your dress off. Now." His commanding voice dripped with the promise of sex.

"Pretty assertive there for a guy trapped to the ground by buttercups."

"But you know as soon as I get out of this botanical prison, you'll be at my mercy, and I will touch you until you beg me to fuck you."

Already at his words, heat pulsed between my legs. I wanted to feel his masterful fingers at the apex of my thighs, but I also wanted to draw this out.

I flicked my fingertips again, and more strands of buttercups slid over his skin, trapping him to the earth.

I leaned down, stroking his face. "An angel, trapped in dirt like a beast." I nipped at his lower lip, my nipples hardening. "How delightful."

His body tensed beneath me. "As long as you keep your legs wrapped around me, I'm happy to be here."

My body reacted powerfully to him, core throbbing. I kissed him more deeply, and his tongue stroked against mine. I rocked my hips on top of him, and I felt as if my body was swelling with heat. The fabric of my dress felt too hot now, and my brain was screaming at me to pull it off. I complied, and the cold night air whispered over my skin. I leaned down again, my nipples grazing his chest, and I kissed him deeply. I rocked my hips against him, moaning.

"Ruby," he breathed, his voice husky. "I need you now." He yanked his wrists against the plant manacles.

I whispered in his ear, "First, I want to hear you say my plant powers are worth exploring."

His hips moved underneath me. "Is this really necessary?"

I brushed my fingertips over his waistband "Say it."

"They're worth exploring."

I leaned in, my body pressed against his, and I started kissing his neck. My tongue flicked over his skin, and I moved my body into his.

He groaned.

"Not good enough," I said. "Tell me you were wrong when you said my buttercups wouldn't do it. My magic is powerful. I should be worshipped.... You know. The kind of stuff Metatron would want to hear."

"Can we not talk about my father right now?"

"Say it."

"I was wrong. You are a goddess of plants and all other things, and I bow before you and worship you in all your magical glory. And, in particular, right now I'd like to worship your perfect curves and your mouth and your breasts and every other part of your body."

Sounded good to me. "Fine." I raised my hands, beckoning the plants toward me. They whipped off his body, freeing him.

Just as I'd anticipated, it had taken my restraining him to entice him to truly unleash himself. He snarled, and in one swift movement, he had me on my back in the grass. Already, he was tugging down my panties, desperate for me. I tore his pants off him, and he lunged for me—more beast than I was at that moment.

He kissed me deeply, and with every thrust of his tongue, my legs fell open a little wider, my back arching. We kissed with abandon, his tongue stroking mine. We were frantic for each other, desperate. From underneath, I rocked my hips against him. He slid into me, and I moved in tune with him until my mind fractured with pleasure.

❧ 28 ☙

Alex and I stood at the edge of a crowd of humans, watching as Rosalind transformed them. Tendrils of her brightly colored magic snaked into the crowd, curling over the humans. Over the course of the past few hours, Rosalind had honed her ability to transform people. Now, she could reach several of them at a time. I stared as her magic curled around a human male, transforming his emaciated and stooped form into a powerful, silver-horned demon.

I glanced up at the shield, hearing the faint thuds of arrows raining against it. Pieces of the shield chipped and flaked off, and my body tensed.

With each direct hit, the cracks in the shield deepened further. At every faint thud, my heart lurched. Each point of contact meant we were one heartbeat closer to death.

My chest felt tight. "Whatever happens, things are about to change," I said to Alex.

"Good." Alex looked up at the shield arching above us. "How much time do you think we have till the Host come through that?"

"I honestly don't know. We're going to try to strengthen

it, and I think I might have an idea of how to do that. But all of this magic is new to me."

"I don't know if we'll survive this," said Alex, "but I know I can't live like a hunted, starving animal anymore. I think death is better than the life I've had in the past year. Whatever happens next, I'm not going back to the rookeries."

I studied Alex for a moment. "What happened to you since I last saw you? Where are Lucy and Katie?"

"What happened to us? More of the same. More starvation, more watching people die. More disease around me. We live, we die. The horsemen toy with us, just like Famine did when he put me on that scaffold. And scaffold or not, all of us humans are just inches away from death in this world. Lucy and Katie are fine, though. They're living in an abandoned mansion right now."

"The last time I saw you—I mean before the resistance started—I was pointing an arrow at you. What was that like? Being abducted, nearly dying, then set free again?"

Alex folded his arms, moonlight washing over him. "I had no idea what the hell was going on when Johnny kidnapped us. We were just cooking our rats over a fire on our rooftop. I didn't even see him coming, just felt this insane hunger ripping me apart." He dropped my gaze, looking over my shoulder. "The hunger nearly drove me mad. I just kept thinking about how I could eat Katie, that she had some meat...." He blinked. "You know what? Never mind. Let's not finish that thought. Anyway, we all blacked out from extreme hunger, and next thing I know, I'm on a scaffold and you're pointing an arrow at me."

"You must have been terrified."

He scrunched his forehead. "Not really. I had no idea what was going on or why you were standing next to Famine, but I knew you'd never even consider shooting me."

Right. Probably best that I leave out the part about how I had, in fact, considered shooting him. "Of course, it never even crossed my mind. And the good news is, Johnny's dead now. I made his head explode. Then what happened to you once Adonis took you away from here?"

"The death angel led us out of the city to an abandoned mansion in Northamptonshire. But I couldn't stay there with just the three of us. We were safe, but in total isolation. They were driving me mad, until I felt like I had nothing to live for anymore anyway. I came back to London, found the resistance, and joined up."

Something tingled over my skin, and it took me a moment to realize it was Rosalind's overwhelming magic, vibrating through the air.

I stared as her colored magic whirled off her body. Within the crowd, she was transforming a middle-aged woman. Before my eyes, the woman's graying, frizzled hair transformed into sleek brown curls, her body growing taller. Shimmering, silver wings grew from her shoulder blades. This frail human woman was turning into a valkyrie, a being that could ride the storm winds and rain death from above.

"Have you chosen what you're going to transform into?" I asked Alex.

"Incubus."

My eyebrows shot up. "Incubus. Really."

"They're gods of sex. Why would I choose anything else? I haven't gotten any action since the Great Nightmare began, but...." He peered into the crowd. "With some of those cute valkyrie ladies wandering around, I'm liking my chances as an incubus."

I nudged him with my elbow. "I have no doubt that you'll be knee-deep in a bit of the ol' how's-your-father soon," I said, trying out the British expression.

Alex grimaced.

"Yeah, that's creepy. Forget I said that."

"I'll pretend it never happened." Another arrow slammed into the shield, showering us with glimmering shield particles, and he frowned. "Do you honestly think we're going to get our army together in time?"

I closed my eyes, thinking of the buttercups and the Milky Way. "I might have a plan. And I think we need to institute it *now*."

AT THE NORTHERN EDGE OF THE DOMED SHIELD, I STOOD by Adonis's side. To our right, Rosalind and Caine were frowning at their work, running fingertips over the cracks.

Apparently, it was news to both of them that they were fallible.

"This doesn't look good," Rosalind grumbled.

"Whatever happens," said Adonis, "we can't fight them here. An open battle against the Host would be suicide. They outnumber us, and their skill level outmatches our forces. They're all trained soldiers. But the Heavenly Host is used to a particular way of fighting. They march in formation. They've always done so. It's their vulnerability."

I nodded. "Our best chance at fighting them is guerrilla-style. We'll need to hide around the City of London, taking cover in some of the ruined buildings and towers. From our hidden vantage points, we can take shots at them with poison-tipped bullets and arrows. Metatron's chaos will be able to eat our weapons, destroy the buildings, everything around us. Even our soldiers, if we let them get close enough. I'm going to try to combat that as best I can. But we'll all have to do our best to stay hidden, so he doesn't know where to strike."

Caine's eyes gleamed like stars in the darkness. "And how are we supposed to fight this chaos power of his?"

"I'm working on it." I tapped my fingertip against the shield. "And this is our first test. When we go into battle with them, we need it to be on our terms, or we have no chance."

Rosalind let out a long breath. "They're going to smash through this any minute now."

Caine crossed his arms. "And you think that our combined magic can be strong enough to make the shield last."

"I have no idea," I said. "But it's worth a shot. I want to try to strengthen the shield with the Divine Order of the Old Gods—all four of us working together. Let's see what happens, okay?"

By my side, I could already feel Adonis's power intensifying, that forceful, dark magic that licked up and down my skin. He began chanting in Angelic, and I tuned out the words. His native language only distracted me.

I glanced at Caine and Rosalind, and the thin strands of magic that curled off their bodies. They closed their eyes, and Caine moved closer to his wife, slipping his arm around her waist. They seemed completely in tune with each other, their magic blending harmoniously, as if they'd done this a million times.

Already, I could see tendrils of their magic sliding over the shield, strengthening it. It spread over my body, raising goosebumps on my skin. Caine's magic was cold and electrifying at the same time, and it tingled up my spine. Rosalind's was almost overpowering—a heady mixture of the seven gods twining together, vibrating through my chest, my bones.

But we needed more to combat the chaos. We needed order. And with any luck, my ancient magic would be exactly what we needed.

I closed my eyes, tuning into the nature around me. Clematis and wild grapes grew on the oaks around me. Grapes ... the forbidden fruit from the Garden of Eden. It seemed fitting enough.

My mind filled with visions of the bright green Garden of Paradise, the burbling river.

In my phantom world, I found my way to a tree wrapped in grapevines—the forbidden tree of knowledge. I stroked my fingertips over the leaves. Patterns and perfect, ordered spirals whirled around me, until I started to realize that I wasn't alone here in my phantom world.

Now, within the garden, the four of us stood around the Tree of Knowledge—completely naked. My eyes roamed over Adonis, Caine, Rosalind—their perfect bodies pulsing with sensual magic. Adonis's powerful hand slid around my waist, his muscled body pressing against mine, pinning me to the tree. His mouth found its way to my neck. My back arched, warmth pooling in my body. My heart raced. Vines twined around our ribs, bringing the four of us together—

When I opened my eyes again, I found grapevines threading into the magic that slid over the shield. The vines had found their way into the cracks and fissures, sealing them shut. In fact, we now stood below an enormous dome of grape leaves.

"Holy shit." Rosalind smiled. "It worked! Are those grape leaves? What in the world...?"

Adonis traced his fingertips over the shield. "Ruby, you have channeled the magic of the Old Gods to perfection. It's the perfect antidote to Metatron's chaos."

"You had a vision. An ecstatic state." Caine's head was cocked, and he was studying me with those keen, pale eyes. "What did you see in your vision?"

I shifted uncomfortably. "Me? Nothing. Just leaves."

He arched an eyebrow. He didn't believe me. As an incubus, he was immediately tuned into sexual energy, which was mortifying. The gorgeous bastard was probably feeding off it right now.

"It's not important," I added. "The important thing is

that we've bought ourselves time so we can finish building our army, and attack them on our own terms."

Another arrow thunked against the shield. This time, it bounced off harmlessly.

Apart from his piercing eyes, Caine practically blended into the darkness around him. As a grandson of Nyxobas, he wore night like a cloak. "If you want to truly catch them by surprise, we can attack at night. I'll make sure shadows hide us, so they'll never see us sneaking into the city."

"When do you want us to sneak into London?" asked Rosalind.

"Metatron has pledged to begin his attack in two days," said Adonis. "Before dawn breaks, we'll sneak into the city and wait for their march."

"When I interrogated Metatron in the Tower," I said, skimming over the details, "I learned the Host will be marching up Tower Hill first, then Minories and Aldgate High Street. We can hide ourselves all over East London, just northeast of the Tower. Alex and I spent enough time in that neighborhood to know which buildings are stable. I know we can't kill the Host, but the poison-tipped weapons will lay them out for a while. When I've mastered the power of the Old Gods, I'll send them all back home again."

Adonis was studying me closely. "The magic of the Old Gods is supposed to be able to counteract angelic magic. If you can find a way to break down Metatron's immortality spell using your light magic, I can destroy his entire army at once. An army of mortals before me doesn't stand a chance. Angelic bodies would litter the streets of London." His eyes looked a little too delighted. "Metatron's army would be reduced to ashy piles of corpses—"

I held up a hand. "I get it, Death, my love, but I'm not sure. I don't think I can use that kind of magic yet." Without dying. "I just don't have enough control."

Rosalind crossed her arms, staring at us. "You guys are kind of a weird couple. I like you, but you're weird."

But Adonis's stormy eyes were still on me. "If it comes down to it, Ruby, you have to use whatever powers are at your disposal. We won't get a second chance at this. And if we lose, we all die."

His words sent a shiver up my spine. He had a point.

❧ 29 ❧

We stood outside Hotemet Castle. With the shield's new vines blocking out most of the moonlight, our world had fallen into darkness, so Adonis had created glowing orbs to give us a bit of light. They now hovered above the army of demons, casting a golden glow over them.

I hugged myself tightly. Adonis and Rosalind had already taken off. Right now, they were on a reconnaissance mission, looking for traps and patrols around the City of London before our arrival.

Before she'd left, Rosalind had transformed our forces from a horde of emaciated humans into something quite terrifying. Along with their demonic bodies came demonic magic. They could now shoot arrows with precision and fly above the angelic forces. Each of them had a weapon laced with Devil's Bane.

Granted, Metatron could break all those weapons apart. But it would be my job to keep it all together.

I scanned the army, my gaze trailing over Alex, whose dark incubus wings swooped behind him. His pupils twinkled like a night sky. For a moment, I felt a chill looking at him—until he broke into his charming smile.

Hazel sidled up to me, then jabbed me with her elbow. "If you can make the angels mortal again, I can burn them all to death with Uthyr."

I shook my head. "If I had time to practice, I could make them all mortal, but I don't think it's going to happen today. The Old Gods only care about one thing: ridding the earth of the horsemen. When I use the light magic, Adonis might end up dead, or anything could happen. The best we can do for now is lay them out with Devil's Bane until I can get some mastery over the situation."

She glared at me. "You realize what happens if you take on Metatron and fail, right? Everything dies."

"Great pep talk—thanks, Hazel." I bit my lip, and a quiet fear clenched my chest. "Anyway, I won't let that happen. I'm not going to let you die." She didn't need to know the consequences right now. I just felt the need to reassure my little sister. "It will be fine, Hazel. I won't let anything bad happen to you. I just want you to stay here, behind the shield."

"That's stupid. I should be circling the city with a fire-breathing dragon, but instead we're supposed to rely on your plants."

"My plants fixed the damn shield. Anyway, you're sixteen, Hazel. You're staying behind the shield." I took a deep breath. "You're breaking my concentration right now."

"What are you trying to concentrate on? Making grass grow in preparation for the big battle? Must be exhausting."

I shot her a dirty look. "I have to convince this entire army of angel-hating former humans that they need to follow Kratos's orders. They agreed to transform into demons, but they don't yet know they're supposed to follow the Hunter."

"Why does it have to be him? I could lead them just as easily. On my dragon."

"He's Conquest, Hazel. He was made for this. He can mentally command thousands of soldiers. He can coordinate it all to perfection."

"So just tell them if they don't follow his commands, they'll probably die."

"I can't just tell them that. It has to be sophisticated. Like a whole inspiring battle speech performance."

She narrowed her eyes at me. "Fine. I'm going inside now. Have fun with your grass magic."

I loosed a long sigh, looking up at our shield. With the plants threaded through it, the shield now blocked us completely from the angels' view. No cherubs or sentinels or any other celestial creatures could see us.

Still, we had to march from here into London, and that meant leaving our dome of protection.

I turned back to the army of demons, and my gaze landed on Lila. The resistance leader was crossing toward me. She looked much the same as before, except now she had delicate wings that swooped from her back. Valkyrie seemed a fitting species for her.

"So, Ruby," she said. "Are you ready to give your little speech to tell them how well you know Kratos, and that he's actually loving and sweet and all that?"

I shook my head. "Not even remotely ready. Dancing is more my thing than speechmaking, and I honestly have no idea what to say. But I'll put on a good show if I can."

I crossed to the tree stump and climbed onto it, staring out at the sea of demonic faces before me. The thing was, burlesque was generally a silent affair. Dancing, fans, sequins, tassels. We weren't known for our oratory skills. But maybe I could borrow from some of the most inspiring speeches I vaguely remembered from history and English class.

I raised my hands. "Friends. Demons. Countrymen! Lend me your ears, for I have come to...." I couldn't remember how the rest of that went. "I have come to tell you that, they may kill us, but they'll never take our freedom!" That made no sense. If we were dead, we wouldn't be particularly free. "We shall fight on the beaches."

I cleared my throat. Not my best performance.

"Okay, look. You all want to live, right?" My voice boomed over the crowd. "We are facing an army of immortal angels with superior skills to ours. Kratos is a living embodiment of the concepts of conquest and victory. If he doesn't lead us, we'll probably die." I scratched my cheek. "Oh, yeah, and he will issue those commands in your mind, so if that happens, it's not a hallucination. Just do what he says."

The crowd of demonic soldiers began murmuring. I could feel the tension rippling off them in waves, the air buzzing with nervous energy.

I glanced at Lila, raising my eyebrows, and she shrugged.

"So, are we good? Please don't tell me I have to show you more images of your deaths at Aereus's hands, because I'm getting a little tired of that."

I raised my arrow. A sword really would have been better, but I didn't have one.

"Give me liberty, or give me death!"

I nodded, and a few sad claps broke the silence. I was dying up here.

At the front of the line of troops, Alex raised his sword, his dark wings swooping from his shoulder blades. "We can't stay within this shield, or we'll starve. We can't leave the shield without fighting back, or the angels will kill us by tomorrow morning. Just get us through this night alive. We'll worry about the rest later."

I turned, smiling at Kratos. I gave him the "thumbs up" symbol.

Okay, one more try. Maybe what they needed was a little more hope. If their lives were only despair and gloom, there wasn't much to fight for. *Put on a good show, Ruby. Give them something to love.*

I raised my arrow. "We're at the precipice between life and death right now. We have been since the Great Nightmare began—fighting for life among the ashes. We are going to war today for the people we love, and that love will give us strength. Our enemies love no one but themselves, and that gives us the advantage. So, when we're done, when we finally rid the earth of the angels who don't belong here, we will rebuild. We will plant fruit trees and vegetables. We will construct our homes again. We will find love and life in the ashes of death."

Silence greeted me, but I think I'd gotten through to them that time, and no one was arguing.

The golden light of the orbs glinted off Kratos's body, gilding him. Wordlessly, he took to the skies above the troops. Now, bestowed with an army, his body seemed to glow even more powerfully, his head burning with a halo.

Move to the portal. Already, I could hear him issuing commands in my mind, his voice deep and booming. Being able to fragment attention, to think about a thousand different things simultaneously, must be some kind of angelic ability.

Meet Caine there. Prepare to open it on my command.

❧ 30 ❧

Caine and Kratos flanked me as I stood before the shield, running my fingertips over it. As I touched it, the shield whirled in a spiral like the Milky Way.

I glanced at Caine. "You can help me open up a portal in the shield, right?"

"Everything except that wall of leaves you created."

"I'll handle that part."

For the first time, I saw Caine with his wings—beautiful, black-feathered wings that blended in the shadows behind him. "Adonis is ready for us. The streets of London are clear of angelic patrols. Metatron isn't expecting us. As the army slips out of this portal, they'll be cloaked with my shadows. The angelic patrols won't be able to see us at all."

My heart beat a rapid tattoo in my chest. "Good."

I ran my fingertips over the shield again, then met Caine's gaze. "Okay. Let's do this, incubus."

He closed his eyes, and his electric magic tingled over my skin, raising the hair on the back of my neck. I felt my back arching at its power.

Then, I pressed my palm against the shield, envisioning a hole opening within the leaves. I could feel their spirits melding with mine, their vibrations tuning into mine. The leaves whirled away from my fingertips, opening a portal in the shield.

Lead them through the portal. Kratos again.

My footsteps crunched over the leaves, and I listened to the rhythmic marching of the demon army behind us. Kratos somehow had us all marching in time with one another. As we moved deeper into the woods, Caine's shadows clung to me, whispering over my skin.

In silence, we moved through the forest, slipping through the trees. This was how the High Fae had once fought—firing arrows from behind the cover of trees. Silent, unseen by the enemy. Humans had a term for the sudden blood clots or paralytic seizures that plagued some of the elderly among them: strokes. That came from us—the fae. In the old days, we hid behind trees, shooting arrows into humans who'd wandered into our territory. A fairy-stroke.

And that's how we'd be taking on the angels today, using the ancient way of the fae. If it went well, they'd be struck down by unseen forces, unable to fight back.

Metatron would try to rip the world apart, and I just had to keep it together.

Caine and I led the troops deeper into the forest. I turned to him as we walked. "Are you worried about what could happen to Rosalind?"

His gaze was icy. "No. She has the power of seven gods. Why? You're worried about your horseman, aren't you? He's the embodiment of death. I don't think you need to worry."

No point lying when we were facing the possible end of the world. "Yeah, but I'm worried about him anyway."

"I thought you were the only person who could kill him."

"That's one of the things I'm worried about. If I have to use the full extent of my powers, Adonis could die. The Old Gods want to rid the earth of the horsemen."

"You're glamoured. You look like a human. A creature who wants to be human can't wield the power of gods."

"What?"

"I'm a demon. Half-incubus. I know what I am. I seduce, and I kill, and my powers are mine. Do you know who you are?"

At his words, I felt unsteady, like the world was tilting beneath my feet, and my heart began to beat a little faster. "Succubus, fae, human, dancer, spy." My answer didn't seem quite as satisfying as it had before.

His glacial eyes shone in the darkness. "And what do you feel when you try to use the gods' power?"

"My feral side comes out. Canines. Blood. Wrath. The whole nine yards."

"You're scared of your feral side. You're repressing it. That's why it takes over when you use the gods' power."

My pulse began to race, and I started to find myself annoyed. "What are you, some kind of demonic therapist?"

"Don't think I don't notice you trying to deflect what I'm saying."

For just a moment, my mind flashed with a memory I wished I'd kept hidden. My teeth, tearing into my mother's flesh. I'd left her permanently scarred. Scared of me, even. "My feral side is scary. Of course I'm scared of it. You should be, too, quite frankly."

"There are angels, and there are beasts. Creatures like us are in between, and you won't control your powers until you accept both sides of yourself. If you fight your feral impulses, they'll take over. The Old Gods can sense your weakness, and they will gain control. Believe me—I've fought the same battle with the God of Night. My powers came from him, but they're mine, now, and I wield them how I want."

AFTER MARCHING FOR HOURS THROUGH THE DARKNESS, we'd finally arrived in the City of London. Kratos's commands guided each of us into the city.

Separate from the rest. Move north. As we moved further south, toward the Tower, Conquest's voice boomed in my mind.

With a nod to Caine, I slipped away from the rest of the demonic horde.

You'll join Adonis, said Kratos.

The Horseman of Conquest still hoped I'd be able to destroy the immortality spell. If I could, Adonis would be at my side to slaughter them all within moments. I only wished I had more time to prepare until I was sure I could take them down.

I moved quietly through London's abandoned streets, following Kratos's directions. As I got closer to Adonis, I broke into a run, desperate to see him.

There's a tall, glass building to your right, said Kratos. *The door is open. Push through it.*

Once again, I had to marvel at Kratos's ability to multi-task, each of us getting our own unique commands.

You'll join Adonis on the top floor.

I pushed through the door, finding myself in a dark stairwell. A few streams of moonlight shone through the doorway, glinting off shattered glass on the floor. It smelled faintly of rotting food in here. In the humid stairwell, I blew a strand of red hair out of my eyes.

While I climbed the dark stairs, I thought back to what

Caine had said. Maybe he had a point. If I was going to take on the power of a god, I couldn't run from myself.

On the one hand, transforming, performing, putting on a show—that was all part of who I really was. But Caine was right, too. I was hiding a part of myself, one that I hardly ever showed to anyone. I hid my ears, my hair. I hated my feral side, and maybe I didn't want to be fae. I wanted the grace and elegance of angels.

I heaved a deep breath. If I was going to use the magic of the natural world, I couldn't reject it.

As I climbed another flight of stairs, I let the glamour shimmer away from my body. My true color.

I let the gemstones glow in my forehead. When I caught a glimpse of myself in the reflection of a door window, I saw my pointed ears sticking through pale, blond hair.

I could adapt, I could change, but I couldn't run from myself. Not if I wanted to wield true power.

Push through the door to your right, said Kratos in my mind.

How did he even know where I was? I was hidden in a darkened, abandoned building, and he seemed to know my every move.

I pressed through a heavy fire door, and a cold wind whispered through a shattered window. A few rays cast pale, silver light over the room. In the dim light, it took me a moment to find Adonis, until he said my name. I caught the gleam of his eyes. He sat by a broken window in the darkened room, the floor littered with bits of debris.

In the darkness, I could just barely see him smiling at me. "Ruby. The real Ruby."

I returned his smile. "We're fighting fae style today. So fae Ruby is here to kick some angel ass."

"I wouldn't want to spend the possible end of the world with anyone else."

I crouched next to him. "Let's try to be a little optimistic and imagine that it's not ending."

I knelt next to the window, taking care to avoid the shattered glass, and I peered out the broken window. Nothing seemed to move in the streets except a few drifting pieces of crumpled paper. The resistance's forces were well hidden, cloaked by tendrils of Caine's night magic. In the quiet darkness, a chill rippled over my skin.

🎕 3 1 🎕

Despite the stillness, around the eastern edge of the old City of London, our soldiers were taking shelter in the rookeries and derelict tower buildings. Just like the old fae, the resistance was waiting to strike unseen—deadly, stealthy arrows and bullets would fly from the shadows.

I took a shuddering breath, meeting Adonis's gaze. The truth was, we didn't fully understand Metatron's powers, and I wasn't sure how long we'd have to attack his forces. I had to face the fact that chaos could take over before we had a chance to fight back. If it did, we could find ourselves ripped apart in the black hole of Metatron's magic.

Adonis reached for me. "You want me to be optimistic, but I can hear your heart racing with fear." He pulled me to his chest, and I could hear his heart beat, too. "Don't let death scare you, Ruby."

I wanted to stay like this forever, wrapped up in Adonis's arms. Or in our forest paradise. "I'm not ready for it to end yet," I said.

"Then let's try to make sure it doesn't."

His body tensed, and he released me. Then he crouched before the window, and I knelt by his side.

"I feel him now," he said. "I feel his magic."

The hair began to stand up on my nape. I felt it now, too, my body reacting to Metatron's otherworldly magic.

I readied my arrow, pointing it out the shattered window. Right now, thousands of us had our weapons trained through glass shards, ready to fire. Guns, arrows, grenades stuffed with shrapnel and Devil's Bane—we'd come well prepared.

Nausea turned my gut—a mixture of nerves and a reaction to Metatron's magic. My hands had begun shaking, and I tightened my fingers on my bow and arrow.

Overhead, the sky began transforming from midnight velvet into a bruise purple until streaks of red spread across the canopy.

My pulse began to race, and the Old Gods' magic simmered in my blood. Fear whispered through me. Distantly, the sound of marching trembled over the streets.

"They're coming," said Adonis from my side.

A few rays of light heralded the oncoming Heavenly Host. As their feet hammered against the pavement, I watched the stream of angels march up Minories. Then, just above his soldiers, soared Metatron himself. His ivory wings beat the air. Golden light radiated from his powerful body, and I found myself unable to tear my eyes away from him.

At any moment, the resistance would begin to attack.

Deep within my skull, Kratos's voice rumbled. *Resistance, prepare to fire. Ruby, ready your magic.*

I forced myself to rip my gaze from Metatron. My breath was coming in short, sharp bursts. As the legion moved closer within range, I set my sights on a broad-shouldered angel at the front of the legion, whose ginger hair flowed down his back. His enormous white wings spread out behind him.

A cold sweat broke out over my body. As soon as we

unleashed our arrows, Metatron would know we were here. He'd start ripping all of this apart with his magic. I had no way of knowing just how rapidly he could destroy a city.

Fire! Kratos's voice rang out like a bell in my mind.

Adonis and I loosed our arrows, and mine found its mark, right in the ginger angel's chest. At the same time, a hail of gunfire rang out, and explosions rocked the streets below. Smoke billowed into the air.

In our minds, Kratos kept commanding us to fire.

As poisoned-tipped bullets rained down on the Heavenly Host, I unleashed another arrow. Chaos ripped apart the army beneath us as the resistance hammered them with Devil's Bane. Through the haze of smoke, I couldn't even see Metatron.

So far, this was working beautifully.

Just as I was reaching into my quiver for another arrow, Metatron's voice rumbled over the horizon.

The Angelic words clanged in my mind, and I squeezed my eyes shut, trying to block out the anarchy. Words and pieces of words whirled around my mind, confusing me. *Buttercup, the brick, zebrek, manifold, lurking, crepusc, melaton, urge....*

Angelic was Adonis's native language, and it didn't seem to affect him. He just kept firing his arrows.

"Ruby," he said. "We need your power. He's starting to pull down the buildings."

I forced my eyes open and looked out the windows. What I saw sharpened my thoughts.

Metatron had simply begun tearing down the buildings where resistance members were hiding. Plaster, cement, and glass crumbled and fractured off the towering buildings around us. If this went on much longer, Metatron would bury the entire resistance in rubble.

I lowered my bow, tuning into the spirits of the plants

that I could connect to around me. It wasn't much: grass, weeds, some clover—but I could use these plants as my own legion.

I let my body meld with their vibrations, their patterns, the divine order of their leaves and blades. Once I felt them responding to me, I commanded them to grow into the buildings, through the brick, through the glass. I sent them rushing through the steel, surging into stone. They sealed the materials together with perfect strength.

Ruby. Kratos's voice in my mind. *The streets just to your north are falling to pieces.*

I tuned into them, to the plants growing there, and I willed them to grow and to bind.

Still, the Heavenly Host were rallying. Those who'd survived the initial onslaught were taking to the air, trying to hunt down the snipers.

"The resistance are panicking," said Adonis from my side. "I can feel the raw fear of all the demons around us. And if they're panicking, they won't be thinking clearly."

Metatron's Angelic language rattled through my skull, and confusion danced in my skull.

Multitude, nurser, milget, rubbe....

Forget the demons. *I* was panicking.

He glanced at me. "I can hear your heartbeat. Everyone needs to stay calm if we're going to win this."

Like air breathing in and out of a bellows, dark magic pulsed from his body. Already, it soothed my mind and washed over my body in calming waves until I could think clearly again.

With my senses sharpened, I summoned another wave of plants, and grasses surged through the buildings' structures.

Gunfire and explosions rocked the streets, and dust clouded the air. Angelic soldiers took to the skies, wings furiously beating, searching for their attackers. But they weren't used to fighting unseen forces like this. We weren't playing by the rules of celestial warfare, and they had no idea how to handle it.

Through the smoke, I couldn't see Metatron, but I could see the angelic bodies littering the streets—burnt and tattered wings, blood staining the pavement. In the air, Metatron's soldiers frantically tried to ferret out the snipers' locations, but they made easy targets. It seemed our plan was actually working.

We were actually ripping apart the Heavenly Host.

While my plants sprouted from the earth, Metatron's magic began echoing around me, reverberating in my skull until nothing meant anything anymore.

Igloo, butters, legitro, melkan, resist, resist, resist—

I couldn't see where he was, couldn't fight back against him, but his magic kept intensifying. I clamped my hands over my ears. Metatron was the black hole at the center of the galaxy, and he was dragging us into his chaos. "Adonis! He's going to rip this world—!"

Before I could finish the sentence, a wave of his powerful celestial magic slammed into us. Glass shattered around me, and the steel began to warp. Panic climbed up my throat, and I screamed for Adonis, reached for him.

My fingers grasped at air, at smoke, and I felt myself falling through debris, an avalanche of shattered glass and plaster raining around us. For just a moment, Adonis's powerful arms grasped me in the air, the scent of myrrh blanketing us. He'd broken my fall, his wings slowly beating the air. Then, his body tensed as something slammed into us. With horror, I stared at the arrow protruding from his neck, the blood pouring from his wound.

He dropped his grip on me, and I felt myself falling.

32

I slammed against rocky debris, and the fall knocked the wind out of me. Dust darkened the air above me, and I drew a ragged breath, filling my lungs with particles of plaster. Adonis's rescue attempt actually *had* saved me—I hadn't fallen too far to the ground, and I'd ended up on top of the rubble instead of buried beneath it.

Still, I was exposed here, and panic began climbing up my throat. I pushed myself up as fast as I could, frantically scanning for Adonis. Clouds of dust from fallen buildings filled the air around me, and I could hardly see a thing. Worse, my bow had been smashed to pieces in the fall.

I can't let Metatron get him. I can't let them take Adonis....

A sharp pain slammed into me from the back, and I fell forward on my hands. Jagged debris bit into my palms. Pain screamed through my shoulder. I glanced down at an arrow tip protruding near my collarbone.

With a trembling hand, I reached behind my back, my fingers grazing the shaft of an arrow lodged in my shoulder blade. Even if I had the strength, I wouldn't be able to yank it out where it had struck. Was I going to die here on my hands and knees?

Shaking, I turned my head to look at my attacker. An angel towered over me, pointing an arrow at me through the clouds of dust.

The wind toyed with his long, dark hair, and blood streaked his skin. "Are you the one they call the Light Bringer?"

Without waiting for an answer, he unleashed the arrow— this one hitting me in the other shoulder. Pain slammed into me.

As I stared at him, battle fury surged in my blood like molten lava. Time seemed to slow down, and I locked my gaze on him. Now, I could hear my own heartbeat roaring in my ears.

These fuckers wanted to destroy the world. But the truth was, that was too abstract for me to even worry about. What rang the most clearly in my mind was this: if the angels won, they'd be coming for Hazel and Adonis. And I couldn't let that happen. I'd fight for the ones I loved.

My pale hair whipped around my head, and my canines began lengthening.

Blood. The Old Gods wanted angel blood, and I was going to give it to them. I was going to end this now. Wrath flooded my mind as Feral Ruby took over. I couldn't feel the pain anymore.

As the dark-haired angel nocked another arrow, I lunged for him, slamming him to the ground. Instinct took over, and my teeth found their way to his throat. Blood poured from his neck, and his screams brought a smile to my lips. My fist slammed into his cheek, shattering bone, and then I was biting him again. He shrieked as I tore at his flesh.

The ancient fury of the Old Gods screamed in my mind. *Kill them all.*

Angel blood gave me strength. I rose to my knees, then snapped the arrow shafts in my shoulders. Grunting, I pulled out the arrows. I threw them down on the rubble.

From behind, another angel came at me with a sword. I ducked, then slashed at his gut with my claws. Blood sprayed from the wound. He dropped his sword, and I picked it up.

Shiny. Good for angel-killing. I wanted to sink it into angel hearts.

The stones in my forehead were heating up, desperate to rid the earth of this scourge. But there was some reason I couldn't do it, couldn't just give in to the blast of light....

I pivoted as another angel came for me through the rubble. My borrowed sword sliced through his angelic body. His blood smelled sweet to me. A frantic stab of pain—injured shoulders—tried to fight its way into my consciousness, but I pushed the thought out again. *Kill.*

Wild energy ran through my body. I felt at one with the wind and the jagged rubble beneath my feet. I cut my sword through another angelic soldier, glorying in the spray of blood as I severed his head from his neck. This was what I had been made for: a red-toothed beast born to slay angels.

I am blood, moss, bones, and earth, a creature of the damp caves. I am the feet pounding the leaves as you run from me. I am the rhythmic terror of your blood roaring in your ears.

My heart hammered like a war drum, life thrumming through my veins. My canines craved more blood. I couldn't quite remember how to speak, couldn't make the words clear in my mind, but....

Had to find someone here, among the rubble. The man who smelled like myrrh. Gray eyes, dark wings.

From the skies above, an ivory-winged angel swooped down to me, slashing his sword.

He thought I was his prey. He was wrong.

I leapt into the air with the force of a wave crashing on the shore, and I slashed my sword through his neck. A beautiful crimson arc of blood.

Thrust. Kill. Draw blood. Come at me, fuckers. I will eat your hearts.

Their terrified hearts beat rhythmically, melding with their screams in a perfect battle song. They feared the Bringer of Light.

I whirled, my sword finding its way into the next enemy.

Vaguely, through the haze of bloodlust in my mind, I wondered where my lover was. Who he was. Who I was. Beast, or....

There was someone I needed to get to, needed to save.

The man with the red flower around his neck, the man who felt like home....

Around me, demons began climbing out of the rubble. Horns, teeth, wings—monsters, all of them. It took me a moment to remember they were on my side. We were all fighting angels.

My gaze flicked over a beautiful one with night magic—an incubus. He was fighting viciously, slicing his sword in graceful arcs through the angels around him.

Where's Adonis?

As some of my panic subsided, Feral Ruby began to grow quiet. Pain throbbed through my body once again, spearing my shoulder, my chest. The agony I'd been ignoring crashed into me, and I dropped my sword.

Find Adonis. Kratos's voice in my mind.

"Easier said than done!" I shouted. I couldn't see him through the dust, the smoke, the magic whirling around me. Now, tendrils of multicolored magic spooled around me— Rosalind's lethal magic curling around angelic soldiers. Demons from the resistance were climbing over the rubble, attacking the angels along with the magical assault. We still had a chance here.

I stumbled over the rubble, trying to feel for my bond with Adonis, that tug in my shoulder. But one of the arrows had ripped right through his mark.

As I touched my ravaged shoulder, Metatron's voice began blaring in my mind again. Anarchy roiled in my skull. Around me, I watched as our troops' weapons and armor began to flake and disintegrate—swords, arrows, guns, splintering into pieces. He was pulling us apart.

The breath left my lungs. Blood poured from my shoulder wound. I tried tuning into the spirits of the plants around me, to make them germinate in the weapons. But Metatron was speaking again, blocking out my own thoughts with his voice, until only one word pounded in my mind.

Beast. Beast. Beast.

He was mocking me, confusing me. And as he did, the world seemed to be fragmenting, falling to pieces. Parts of buildings, pavement, steel, and glass danced and ruptured in the air around me. And then, another angelic phrase ... *worship me.* It was an answer to the chaos, a beacon in the darkness. He had the answers I needed.

It felt like a command I couldn't ignore. I fell to my knees in the rubble, my hands in the dust, the jagged cement scraping at my skin.

I looked up from the ground, awed to find Metatron. Radiant light beamed from his head.

He spoke to me in my mind.

Ruby. I'm going to tear your mind apart, and your sister will be next. And I want you to die knowing that the man you love will be eternally punished for his transgressions.

His words cleared my mind again. I needed to stop this. I needed to stop it all....

I needed the Old Gods, even if it killed me. Even if they ripped my body apart with the power of their light.

My world tilted. Time seemed to slow down again, and Metatron's dark hair twisted and writhed in the wind. His mouth moved slowly, forming words he used as weapons.

A familiar scent hit me—myrrh. My gaze flicked to Adonis. He was crawling from the rubble, his dark wings coated in dust. His stormy gray eyes locked on me. His armor, his sword began to disintegrate before my eyes. And then, to my horror—even his wings began to fragment. Aereus swooped over him, moving in slow motion, his sword raised.

Unable to get up from my knees, I stared at Adonis, screaming his name. Aereus—the Horseman of War—raised his sword over Death's head.

If I used the magic of the Old Gods, I'd die.

But I didn't have a choice anymore.

As I met Adonis's gaze, light blazed from my body. I gave in to it, relinquishing control. The power of the Old Gods ripped me open, streaming from my ribs, my bones. I felt my lungs and organs expand, and agony fractured my mind.

Even as I fragmented, I could see the world slowly come together again—divine order and light slowly piecing together feathers, metal, stone—one particle at a time. But the magic was overpowering—a stolen force I couldn't control. My back arched, and ancient forces pulled me further apart.

When I looked up at Metatron, in his golden eyes, I saw something new. Something strangely human: fear.

With the last bit of strength in me, I pushed myself to my feet.

I was going to die, but Metatron was coming with me. I grasped his body in an embrace.

And I let the magic of the Old Gods erupt.

33

As the pain left my body, everything around me seemed to crumble into atoms. I watched the world dissolve around me, until darkness replaced it.

I couldn't feel anything, couldn't place myself in space. I had no idea if I'd been here for a few seconds or for an eternity. Time didn't quite make sense anymore.

Until—a burst of light in the darkness.

I could hear my own breathing, my own heartbeat. I was here at the beginning and the end of it all. In the time before words and after them.

Nothing would last forever, and in the end, chaos would eat us all. But Adonis and I—we'd been sparks of light in the darkness.

I felt him here, in fact. I felt his soothing presence, his calming effect on my mind. Death, my lover, was with me, here, and he wanted to bring me back. I reached for him, trying to stroke him, embrace him, but I couldn't find him in the darkness. That light was too far from me. I wanted to feel his smooth skin under my fingertips, and they stroked helplessly through the air. *Nothing.*

Loneliness ate through me, and a rising sense of panic. I couldn't stay here forever on my own, separated from the people I loved.

Then, the distant chink of light expanded, swirling with green in the darkness, until light and matter began to bloom and piece together around me. A solid ground of soil formed beneath my feet.

From the void, a garden formed, until leaves from plants brushed my calves. I took a step, my feet sinking into the soil.

I blinked, my eyes dazzled by the azure sky. Okay, so this was death, and I was in Paradise. Not the worst outcome, I supposed.

Had the Old Gods just taken me here? Maybe they didn't hate me after all, because it seemed fairly heavenly here. In fact, the scent of the garden intoxicated me. Was this Eden?

Yes.

I caught a glimpse of Azazeyl slipping through the trees. This was where it had all begun, where minds had gone to war with bodies, creation with instinct, where the Old Gods had begun to fight the new.

I spotted a tree in the corner of my eye, its trunk wrapped in grapevines. I *needed* to know how the fruit tasted.

I hurried to it, then plucked one of the grapes from the tree. I popped it in my mouth. I bit down on it, and the sweet juice washed over my tongue. I swallowed, and golden, powerful magic spilled through my veins and filled my skull. As it did, I felt my body start to move again. As if by its own volition, my body twirled through the garden, my bare feet skimming across leaves and moss.

Long ago, when I'd danced, my mind had been silent. Peaceful.

Now, as I moved through the garden, perfect silence washed over me. I twirled, extending my arms as I moved. I pointed my toes, lifting my leg into the air. With every graceful arc of my arms, light beamed from my body. It was just like Caine had said. I was an angel and a beast, in a garden of life and death.

As I moved, words began to form in my mind. Angelic words. But now, they seemed like they belonged in my thoughts—like a skill I'd once had and lost, a sense that had once been native to me.

I couldn't run from the past, from the memories I wanted to forget. I couldn't ignore the blood staining my memories, my teeth piercing flesh. My feral side. It was a part of me.

But I could change the way the story was told. I could give it new meaning. Love and rage were primal, animal forces, but we could shape them with our stories.

I caught a glimpse of a perfect form moving through the trees.

Azazeyl?

I moved toward him, his powerful magic drawing me closer. Gray eyes, midnight wings—it wasn't Azazeyl. It was Adonis, his night-kissed magic spooling from his body. I ran to him, and he wrapped his arms around me. I pressed my head to his chest, listening to his heartbeat.

Perfect spirals of magic whirled from him like the Milky Way.

Death, my lover, ruled this domain. But he wanted me back among the living. The smell of myrrh swept over me, raising goosebumps on my skin. I pulled his face to mine, kissing him.

With the kiss, life streamed back into my body.

When I opened my eyes again, I found myself in Adonis's arms.

Back in London, in a cloud of dust. Life suffused my body. He'd healed me completely, and I felt amazing. I stared at the gorgeous planes of his face, wanting to pull him in for another kiss. The sweet music of Paradise still played in my ears.

"You brought me back. Is it over? The battle?" I asked, warmth lighting up my body.

"No."

Well, fuck. That killed the mood. I'd just died, and my death hadn't even finished the job.

All at once, the roaring of battle noises returned to me. The clashing of swords, the agonized screams of people losing limbs. The brutal pounding of my own heart.

"Metatron is gone," said Adonis. "Banished to the Celestial realm by the Old Gods' power. That was your doing, when you grabbed him. But the rest of their army remains. Along with Aereus."

My heart hammered, and I pulled myself free from Adonis's embrace and rose to my feet.

Above us, winged demons were fighting the angels. I caught a brief glimpse of Caine, a blur of silver and black, rushing for an angel, his sword raised in the air.

Ruby. Kratos's voice boomed in my mind once more. *Can you kill Aereus?*

"Working on it!" I shouted.

My gemstones began simmering and tingling. I glanced overhead, where Aereus was locked in a battle with Kratos. They weren't far above us. In fact, I could probably drag War down from here. That fucker had nailed my boyfriend to a wooden plank, and I was still pissed about it.

Already, I could feel the Devil's Bane building in me, curling from my fingertips.

I flung out my wrists, and ropes of the plant spooled out of my body, wrapping around the Horseman of War.

I tugged on the vines, yanking him down to earth. He slammed hard on the rubble, and dust puffed in an enormous cloud around him.

He started to stand, roaring with rage. His very presence ignited wrath in my body. I wanted him to suffer. Strength

223

rippled through me, and I grabbed him by the throat. I squeezed his neck, reveling in the pain etched across his features.

"I have a message. You don't belong here. You never did. Not because you're a horseman. Because you're an evil, stupid fuck who created hell on earth, and you don't even know why."

He screamed, and I lifted my free hand to his face. Devil's Bane spiraled out of my fingernails, surging into his mouth and his eye sockets, his nostrils. My plants ripped through his bones and veins, crawling through his wretched heart and arteries. He gurgled, his skin bulging and ripping apart.

"Your time on earth is over." I flicked my wrist, and his body exploded into particles of flesh and bone.

I glanced at Adonis, whose gray eyes had gone wide. He gripped a sword, ready to cut into more angels, but the sight of me exploding another horseman seemed to have distracted him, and he was giving me that look again, somewhere between horror and admiration.

But he didn't have long to stare, because already an angel was rushing up behind him, sword raised.

Adonis whirled, gracefully slashing his sword through the angel's neck. Headless, the angel fell into the rubble.

When I looked closer at the soldier from the Heavenly Host, I could now see the magical spells writhing in the air around him. The words snaked and curved around every one of them. It was the immortality spell.

I stared as the magic vibrated around the decapitated angel's neck, shimmering until his head appeared again.

Immortal.

Kratos's voice rang in my mind again. *Can you pull the immortality spell off the soldiers?*

It was just that a silver-haired angel was swinging for me. I ducked, and his blade whooshed over my head.

"Working on it!" I shouted again.

I unleashed a stream of Devil's Bane from my fingertips, and it surged into his body, ripping him apart from the inside out.

I glanced at Adonis, who was fighting through the angels around him.

I whirled, trying to keep the oncoming horde off of me. I was dimly aware of Kratos's commands in my mind. He was trying to direct our demonic allies to keep me safe, but there were just so many angels. I shot out another blast of Devil's Bane, and the magic curled around some of the soldiers around me.

Time to make them mortal again.

I arched my back, flinging out my arms. I was a black hole, pulling the golden magic toward me with an overpowering gravitational force.

The golden words spun through the air in perfect spirals that mirrored the Milky Way, ripping away from all of the angelic soldiers.

I pulled the immortality spells off one soldier after another—from the streets and the sky—and they spiraled into me.

As I made the enemy mortal once more, a blaze of fire seared the air above me.

Hazel, on her godsdamned dragon. She was picking off members of the Heavenly Host who flew in the sky. Their mortal bodies burned, and ash rained down from the heavens.

The angelic magic of immortality streamed into my body —words upon words—until I'd ripped every last spell from them.

"Your turn, Death." I glanced at Adonis, who was already rising into the air.

His back curved, as if in ecstasy. A chink of light broke through the clouds, and golden rays washed over him while his wings carried him into the air. He cast an enormous, dark shadow over the city.

Dark magic spiraled off of him in perfect arcs, like the curves of a seashell, and there was something beautiful and terrifying about it at the same time. The magical tendrils slipped over the Heavenly Host, curling around each victim. As soon as it touched them, each of them seized up, their eyes bulging.

Here he was—the bringer of death. His black wings beat the air. I couldn't help it—even if he was the man I loved, right now, he scared the crap out of me. I felt my knees going weak looking up at him. He looked like a god of death, and it was hard to reconcile this image with the Adonis who thought fondly of his garden. Still, it was like he said—we were both destructive monsters, but that wasn't all we were. It wasn't the limit.

I stared at one of the angels who'd been coming for me—a black-haired woman with silver eyes. As Adonis's dark magic spun around her, her skin began to turn purple. She was putrefying before my eyes. Holes formed in her flesh, and the scent of rot rolled off her.

My lip curled. My lover had a very, very disturbing skillset.

I closed my eyes to the horrifying sight before me. When I opened them again, piles of the angelic dead littered the streets.

Among the dead, the demonic forces began moving. I scanned the survivors, relieved every time my gaze landed on someone I cared about.

For just a moment, perfect silence reigned.

❧ 34 ❧

I sank deeper into Kratos's bath—regrettably, without Adonis to keep me company this time.

I'd washed off the ash and blood of battle, although it couldn't, unfortunately, wash the image of the putrefying angels out of my mind. Their bodies now littered the streets. Perfect fertilization for the gardens and fields we needed to plant. We'd be rebuilding this world, one vegetable patch at a time. Already, the members of the former resistance were clearing London's streets of angel bodies. They had begun hauling them out to open fields and razing abandoned buildings to create more farmland.

The resistance had begun and ended in London, and now the entire world could rebuild. It would be a while before we got things back to normal again. Transportation between countries was limited, and we had to rely on growing our own food. Luckily, I could help in that regard.

I toweled off my body, marveling at the pale, golden glow emanating from my legs. The glow of immortality. Truthfully, I felt amazing.

When I straightened again, I nearly jumped out of my

skin. Kratos was standing there in the doorway, his copper eyes locked on me.

"Gods below, Kratos. You need to stop watching me while I bathe."

"Why? I appreciate your beauty."

"It's creepy."

"Is it?"

It had taken me this long to understand that some of Kratos's creepiness was just an inability to understand normal social conventions. "What are you doing here?"

He straightened. "I wanted to thank you for ridding me of my curse."

I pulled the towel tightly around me. "Thank you for leading our army to victory."

"It's what I was born to do."

I smiled. "It's part of what you were born to do. But it's not the limit. You're free now, and you can do what you want." I studied him, his rigid posture of a commander. "What *are* you going to do next?"

I couldn't stop wondering if Kratos had finally gotten laid, but I wasn't going to come out and ask it.

"I'm going to get busy," he said.

"Interesting turn of phrase."

"...with rebuilding the world that I helped to destroy. I've learned that I don't like living in isolation. Humans and demons in London may not accept me, since they remember me as the Hunter. I was tempted to terrify them into submission so that they would accept and love me."

I narrowed my eyes. "That's not really how love works."

"But your human friend Alex suggested I can earn people's trust again by helping to recreate what was lost. After all, conquest isn't just about war. It's about taking over a new place and making it your own. It's about construction as much as it is about destruction."

I nodded. "The ruins of the world could definitely use your help."

His gaze slid over my bare shoulders. "I'd also like to fuck someone." His jaw tightened. "Obviously not you. I mean, I would like to have sex with you, but—"

"Maybe just stop talking."

"Right." He nodded curtly. "Good talk."

"I'll get dressed on my own."

Before leaving, he turned to me one last time. "Do you think you could pull the curse off Muriel? If she were into that kind of thing?"

I loosed a sigh. There was no way around it. I was involved in Kratos's love life.

"I will ask her what she thinks." *Even though she sucks.*

Without another word, Kratos turned and left me alone.

Now, I had some rebuilding of my own I wanted to do. I had spent so long thinking about my phantom life—the perfect vision of a cottage, a garden, a sylvan paradise. Now, I had the chance to try to make it real.

✥ 35 ✥

I hammered another nail into the side of the oak plank. I'd wanted this cottage, dammit, and I was making it myself.

I'd promised the resistance we'd rebuild, and that was exactly what we were doing now. I was making my phantom life real.

It was a little different from my fantasy—not quite the forest. In fact, fields and gardens stretched out around me.

I stepped back from my creation, a smile curling my lips. Adonis had offered to make a cottage with magic—a perfect one, carved with the words of the gods. But I'd wanted to make something with my hands. I'd wanted to feel the wood beneath my fingertips. I didn't want it to be perfect. I wanted the crooked lines and unevenness of the nails. And I wanted it to be a surprise for him, compelled by some primal instinct to make a home for my family.

I took another step back. It was perfect in its imperfections.

Hazel sidled up to me, holding a sausage in her hand. She

stared at the cottage. "Yeah, that thing looks like a piece of crap."

"Thanks, sis."

"You should just stay at Kratos's castle with me."

"This is my paradise," I said. "And you know what? I'm going to eat godsdamn soup in here. You can visit us from his castle."

She bit into her sausage. "Whatever."

Hazel turned to the garden behind us. "Did you make all this?"

I turned to survey my work. A blue river carved through the forest, and red anemones dappled its banks. "It's modeled after the garden where Adonis was born. He hasn't seen it yet."

There were seeds of death, here in Paradise, but that was okay. I rubbed my rounded belly. Death grew in me, too.

Hazel pointed at my stomach. "How's your little deathling?"

I swallowed hard. My mouth had been weirdly watery since I'd gotten pregnant. "It's making me puke three times a day, and I have an uncontrollable urge to eat a vat of soup. But Yasmin keeps telling me that's normal. It's not a horseman-spawn thing."

"Remind me never to get pregnant. I'm going back to the castle. Kratos is making me a gin and tonic. He's never had alcohol before a week ago, and between you and me, I think he likes the sauce too much, if you know what I mean."

I scowled. "I told him you're not allowed to drink."

"Oh, yeah. He said I'm not supposed to tell you." She paused, turning to frown at the cottage. "It's still missing something. I'm not sure what."

I narrowed my eyes at it. She was right. It *was* missing something.

It was missing Adonis's touch.

I crossed to the other side of the cottage. This is where I'd planted the vegetables—potatoes, carrots, cabbage. I was even growing garlic.

The crunching of footsteps through the leaves turned my head, and I smiled at the sight of Alex coming closer.

"I think this garden is a step up from our Bethnal Green garden."

"Want to help me catch some rabbits?" I asked. "I have rabbit stew plans. Adonis doesn't know that stew and soup are basically the same thing, and he's agreed to eat it."

"I don't mind setting some traps. As long as I never have to eat rat meat again."

"You know you're welcome to stay here at the castle. Kratos said it was fine, and he's got a billion rooms."

Alex wrinkled his nose. "I came here to say goodbye. I was fine letting him lead us into battle, because it meant we got to live. I was fine with recovering here. But I don't want to spend any more time around the Hunter than I have to. And anyway, I want to go back and rebuild the city. We have a lot of angel bodies to clear."

"Do you really think London can recover?" I asked.

"My lovely American friend—London is one thing I'm not worried about. Do you have any idea how many times that city has been burnt to the ground completely? Queen Boudicca slaughtered everyone, burnt it to the ground. A seventeenth-century baker lit the whole place up. Nothing remained when the fire was done except ashes and melted bones. The Luftwaffe bombed the ever-loving shit out of it.

"And you know what happened? Every time, Londoners just went back and recreated the same winding, meandering, nonsensical bullshit streets we've been using for two thousand years. We are putting it back exactly like it's always been. We're rebuilding the crooked streets with ridiculous names like Poultry and Crutched Friars. In a few years' time, I could be passing out under pub tables again."

"Passing out under pub tables. Your aspirations are awe-inspiring."

"Hey, we survived all this because we knew how to fanta-size, didn't we? You fantasized about cupcakes—"

"And cottages with soup." And Adonis naked.

"And I fantasized about having fun again. Being irresponsible again. Doing shit just for the hell of it instead of for survival. We survived this because we told stories of the good old days, and for just a few minutes, they felt real to us. Golden-flaked cupcakes, expensive burgers. Burlesque routines. That's why we're alive."

Our lives and souls were defined by the stories we told. "I call that the phantom life."

"What?"

"The life you create in your mind that seems almost as real as this one." I nodded at my vegetable garden. "You haven't had time to plant stuff yet. Take some of this with you. When I go back to London, I'm going to clear that entire field in Bethnal Green."

"The one with our shitty garden?"

"Yeah, except I'm going to make a not-shitty garden."

"Your words inspire me. And I'm taking some potatoes with me because my stomach is about to eat itself."

On the way out of the garden, Alex leaned down, pulling up a few potatoes and stashing them in the crook of his arm. I smiled as I watched him walk between the oaks. I had an overwhelming urge to make sure that man always stayed fed from now on.

I crossed to the potato patch, plucking a few out for myself, and I brushed the soil off them. I had my rabbit, pota-toes, and carrots. Adonis and I would eat by the fire tonight.

Metatron had tried to get into my head, to convince me

that paradise on earth wasn't possible. That a fae like me would always give in to her feral, bloodthirsty instincts. He'd tried to destroy my phantom life.

But I was here, now, and I might be a feral fae with stones in my head who sometimes tried to eat people, but that's not all I was.

⚜

I STIRRED THE STEW, BREATHING IN ITS RICH SCENT.

When the sunlight slanted lower through the trees, casting long shadows over the forest floor, I felt Adonis's presence—his rich, soothing magic that whispered over my skin. It felt like home now. Adonis had been spending his days healing the injured members of the resistance. We'd set up a triage system, and the most severely injured had been healed first.

During the nights, I'd come here to work on my little project.

I'd kept my work here hidden from him, because I wanted to surprise him. Admittedly, the cottage had been for myself.

But the garden outside, the one modeled after his home in Afeka—that was for him. Here, our two worlds could meld together.

I crossed out of the cottage into the vibrant garden outside. I'd built this cottage next to the river on purpose, at the mouth of a cave. The bright blue of the river mirrored the color of the gemstones still embedded in my forehead. Using my plant magic, I'd grown myrrh trees lining the river's edge. And among them, I'd created the blood-red anemones in the tall grasses, just like the one he wore around his neck.

I watched him as he walked along the river's edge, his blue-gray eyes glinting. I felt ridiculously proud of my work.

His dark, sensual magic slipped around me, raising goose-bumps on my skin.

"This is perfect," he said.

I squinted in the dying sunlight. "Not quite perfect, but good enough." I grabbed his hand, leading him into the cottage. "I made us dinner."

"I don't actually need to eat."

"It doesn't matter. You can enjoy life, now, so enjoy it."

We crossed into the cottage, and Adonis swept his gaze over it. "It's beautiful. You made all this?"

"With my bare hands. Except I don't understand things like plumbing and electricity, so someone's going to have to magic that into existence before we stay here overnight."

The stew simmered in a cauldron over the stone fireplace, and Adonis crossed to it.

"Taste it," I said.

He plucked a ladle from the stone mantle and scooped out a small spoonful. When he tasted it, his eyes lit up. "This is delicious."

I beamed. "See? I knew you'd like soup. I mean—stew."

His forehead crinkled. "This is what soup is?"

"Yeah." Once again, I was staggered at how little time he'd spent eating in his two thousand years. I'd be spending the rest of our immortal lives working on changing that. "What did you think it was?"

"I think I had it confused with that dish of mashed fruit and lard."

I gagged. "I don't even want to know what that is."

He took another spoonful. "People eat it all the time. You light it on fire."

I blinked. *"What?"*

"At Christmas."

"Oh, that's Christmas pudding. Only the British eat that. Let's never speak of it again."

I crossed to the stew, stirring it again while the steam curled around me.

Adonis sidled up behind me and rubbed the gentle curve of my belly. "Do you know that I've never seen you look more perfect?" His voice caressed my body. "How's little Thanatos?"

"We're not calling him the Greek word for *death*." I scowled. "Or her."

"It's a noble name. What were you thinking of?"

"Jackson for a boy."

His body went stiff. "Jackson's not even a real name. It's the surname of America's second-worst president."

"Thanatos is not a real name. It's the personification of a rather grim concept."

"It's been my name for several thousand years."

"It's also your horse's name. We're not naming our baby after your horse. You can't just keep calling everyone *Thanatos*."

"Fine." He took another spoonful of the soup. "We'll think of a new name."

"Speaking of names." I turned to face him. "This cottage is missing something. It needs your mark."

"What do you mean?"

"I used my hands to build it. And I used the magic of the Old Gods to cover it in anemones. But it needs something from the angelic world. This is supposed to be our home together."

He pushed a strand of my pale, blond hair out of my eyes. "I think I have an idea."

He crossed outside and stood facing the cottage. He closed his eyes, and he began speaking in Angelic. I still couldn't understand what it meant, but the words no longer bothered me. They sounded beautiful on his tongue. As he spoke, golden Angelic letters etched into the sides of the cottage, beaming out from the wood. When he finished, he opened his eyes to stare at his work.

"What does it say?" I asked.

"It's just our story. You know, beautiful, angelic perfection meets argumentative beast-woman."

I gave him a shove. "Don't make me bring out my feral side."

"You scare me, woman. And I like it."

I stared at the cottage, at the golden words glowing among the ropes of flowers. Here, in our new home, the Old Gods melded with the new.

My phantom world—the stories I'd told myself—had come to life in front of my eyes.

CHAPTER 36

I held Liora up just under her shoulders, trying to coax a smile from her. Mornings were when she smiled the most, before the sounds and noises of the day started to annoy her and she yelped angrily.

"Come on, Liora. You woke me up four times last night. I deserve a smile." The corners of her lips turned up, and I beamed. "That's a smile! That's a good girl! Smile for Mommy!"

A few years ago, if I'd overheard this sickly-sweet tone, I'd have rolled my eyes, and now it was just flowing out of me like spit-up from a baby.

Liora stuffed a pudgy fist in her mouth, gnawing on it. She had her father's stormy gray eyes—almond-shaped, with dark eyelashes—and some of the fattest cheeks I'd ever seen on a baby. Faint, blond wisps grew on her head.

Liora was lucky—born into a world we were rebuilding. With the angelic invasion driven from the earth, we were starting to put the world back together just the way it had been.

I drew Liora in closer to me, sniffing her head. She had that perfect baby smell.

Adonis's footsteps creaked the floor behind me. "See?" He said. "Dirt and moss smells lovely."

From the floor of our cottage, I scowled at him. "That's not what she smells like."

He reached down, picking her up and cradling her in his arms. Light from the morning sun washed over him.

Adonis had lived for two thousand years thinking he was unable to father a child. And he had been, all that time. But when I'd pulled the curse off him, something had changed, I supposed. Death could create life.

I wasn't going to second-guess it, anyway. I had my imperfect paradise here, and I wasn't going to ruin it.

☙❧

THANKS SO MUCH FOR READING OUR BOOKS.

We have a number of series set in the *Demons of Fire and Night World,* including *Vampire's Mage* and *Shadows and Flame.* If you want to be introduced to some of the other characters in our series, you can download our free stories here. https://dl.bookfunnel.com/geobq4cyhg

Also, check out our webpage for the full listing of books www.cncrawford.com

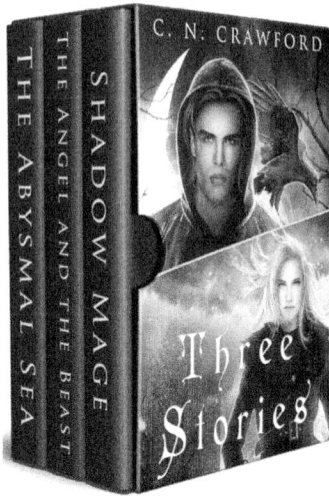

PLEASE JOIN OUR SUPER FUN FACEBOOK GROUP!

ACKNOWLEDGMENTS

Thank you to my lovely beta reader Michael who talks me through all my book crises (and other crises to be honest), and to my editors, Robin and Isabella Jack.

Doc Wendigo, Shayne Rutherford, and Brian Jaramillo contributed their design expertise to our gorgeous ebook and paperback covers.

ABOUT THE AUTHOR

C.N. Crawford is sometimes one person, and sometimes two. We live in Vermont with our son. In this case, *A Spy Among the Fallen* series is written by Christine.

Christine grew up in New England and has a lifelong interest in local folklore—with a particular fondness for creepy old cemeteries. She is a psychologist who spent eight years in London obsessively learning about its history, and misses it every day.

ALSO BY C.N. CRAWFORD

C.N. Crawford has written two other series that take place in the *Demons of Fire and Night* world.

Please Check out the ***Vampire's Mage*** series, and ***The Shadows and Flame*** series for more books in the same universe.

A full listing of our books are found here:

http://www.cncrawford.com/books/

Printed in Great Britain
by Amazon